THROUGH
THE
UNDERTOW

A Son's Journey
of Healing
from Parental
Infidelity

THROUGH
THE
UNDERTOW

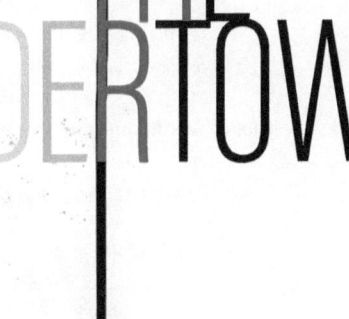

ALICE RAUSCH
NICHOLAS NEWELL

with Katie Henricks

Writers of the Round Table Press
PO Box 1603, Deerfield, IL 60015
www.roundtablecompanies.com

Editor: **Katie Henricks**
Cover Designer: **Sunny DiMartino**
Interior Designer: **Christy Bui**
Proofreaders: **Adam Lawrence, Carly Cohen**

Printed in the United States of America

First Edition: December 2020
10 9 8 7 6 5 4 3 2 1

Library of Congress Cataloging-in-Publication Data
Rausch, Alice.
Through the undertow:
a son's journey of healing from parental infidelity
/ Alice Rausch and Nicholas Newell.—1st ed. p. cm.
ISBN Paperback: 978-1-61066-086-0
ISBN Digital: 978-1-61066-087-7
ISBN Audiobook: 978-1-61066-093-8
Library of Congress Control Number: 2020915237

Writers of the Round Table Press and the logo
are trademarks of Writers of the Round Table, Inc.

This book is dedicated to my dear friend, Margie Phillips, whose love and commitment to her family inspired my own healing. You are so missed and will never be forgotten.

To all who have been betrayed by infidelity and have found the courage to heal through it, this book is for you.

To those of you betrayed who still struggle to overcome the trauma, whether the betrayal was by a parent or partner, this book is for you. Keep healing those wounds.

To the organization Affair Recovery, and to others who are doing tremendous work to help heal betrayal trauma and foster mental and emotional health in this country, this book is for you.

Lastly, to all of you who choose to be faithful and loving to your spouses, this book is for you. Keep demonstrating what real sexiness is. Your spouses, your children, your community, and I appreciate you.

Although this book is a work of fiction, it is based on a true story.

1

CRAZY OR DEAD

This was my dream. I was officially a "plebe," or a freshman, at one of the most prestigious establishments in United States history: the US Naval Academy. I had somewhat of an obsession with military history that never really went away. It wasn't just a fanboy kind of obsession, but a deep desire to be written into its pages, to be part of something bigger. The path wasn't without sacrifice. I had sacrificed a solid social life—my relationship with Paige in senior year—and fought for stellar grades over the last couple of years to earn this type of honor. Not just anyone was accepted to the academy, and I knew it. I also knew that it was where I was supposed to be. I know I'm just nineteen, it's early to know what I want . . . whatever. I'd heard it from practically everyone I told, but it was where I belonged; I could feel it.

Okay, fine. If I were totally honest, I *didn't* know if this is where I belonged. Deep down, I struggled to keep up with the emotional, physical, and psychological rigor of training. Sure, I'd heard the stories, but experiencing them was something completely different. I was perpetually exhausted, pushed to my absolute physical limit, held to Ivy League academic standards, and put under enough pressure to create a diamond from my insides. The looming weight of self-doubt crept over me more times than I care to admit.

That night, I lay in bed wondering if I had what it took to endure this extreme environment that molded heroes and patriots out of normal kids like me. Was I born to be a hero? I began to feel my insides squeeze around my organs. Being away from home and Mom and my brothers, I felt like I was being held together with dental floss and chewing gum, and I couldn't keep up the guise any longer. I did have a sponsor family here. As plebes, we're all assigned a sponsor family as a way to feel supported in our first year away from home. You know, a place to do laundry, enjoy a nice meal, and be with a family, just not your biological one. But even that positive thing just made me realize how dysfunctional my own family had become.

It was winter of my first year at the academy. The past two years had been a train wreck for me. I watched the decimation of the family (and the mother) I once had. The family dinners, the game nights went away, as my family transformed into some morphed, fractured version of itself. The stress of it had begun to take its toll on me. These circles under my eyes were new, and it felt like the lean muscle I once wore like armor had leaked out of me since last year.

I was almost constantly sore. Some days, I woke up and could barely walk. Some nights my arms hung helplessly but were stuck bent inward from soreness, making me look like, as my roommate told me, "a fucking T. rex." I'd never been sore like this before. Even with all the training, I felt weak lately compared to the *machine* I was in the training grounds of the Naval academy, and although no one else could tell besides my roommate, I could. I swore I had the strength and tenacity to keep it up and suffer through plebe year with my game face on, but that's the funny thing about heartache: you can't will yourself out of it.

On this specific morning, I felt like I had come down with the flu, and if it was, it was the worst I'd ever had. I could move my arms but just barely, was nauseated to the core, and my muscles ached. I hobbled out of bed on a prayer and took my morning piss. My arms, in their T. rex pose but now coiled up tightly, barely pulled through the arms of my shirt as I attempt-ed to get dressed. I called for my roommate, Sam, but he was already out the door. I chucked my bag over my shoulder and headed out the door against my better judgment. I felt so weak I had a classmate carry my backpack for me. I couldn't put my finger on what was going on here, but I had a long day ahead of me and I needed to power through.

As I zipped up my school bag after first period, I couldn't escape an even heavier, creeping feeling inside me. I'd made it through first period, but now the pain in my back and stom-ach were almost unbearable. I reached for a deep breath, and then another, but each inhalation after the next felt shallower and shallower, capping out before I got the hit of air I truly needed. I tried again and again and again. I began to panic. My heart raced past any cadence of rhythm. I felt my face fade eight shades. As the lights suddenly penetrated me in a con-suming beam, my lips shriveled into my face like a prune, and in another instant, as my whole body retracted into a frail pile, I hit the tile floor with a thud.

In a way, I felt the childlike innocence bleed out of me in that moment on the floor, never to return again. A crowd of students gathered, hovering over me in concern, as I lay there immobile, staring hard into the blinding lights overhead, dar-ing them to look away first. I was well on my way to crazy or dead; I just wasn't sure which one.

There's not a lot I remember from that moment until I came to in my hospital bed, but there are flashes of things. I remember the lights from every direction. I remember this one geeky kid who sat in the front row of every class standing over me, ask-ing intrusive questions that I couldn't answer. I only stared at him with a blank, confused awareness. There was the abrupt rise and fall of the gurney, and I was thinking how strange-ly comforting the back of an ambulance was: a place to rest.

My name was being repeated several times as my head spun. There was the steady procedure of the EMTs, and a slight drop in my fear as I realized I was in good hands. I was on my way to Walter Reed Medical Center.

I remember the predictable "beep" of the monitors in the background of the frigid ER. A middle-aged Filipina nurse draped a fleece blanket over me while she handed me "something that'll help." I gladly extended my shaky hand as far as it would go and delicately tossed the two white pills from their teeny cup to the back of my throat. Minutes later, I felt the flood of lorazepam coat my brain, and I drew in a long, deep breath for the first time in what felt like a solid year. I sat propped up and sipped lukewarm water out of a miniature Dixie cup. Man, if my dad could see me here, on this stretcher, in this ER. I could feel the anxiety swell back up inside me like a backed-up toilet. This was all his fault.

A doctor in hospital green scrubs, who seemed barely older than me, casually trailed in next to me, closing the curtain with a shrill skim of metal on metal. I always pictured ER doctors to be older white males with cocky attitudes and serious, bass voices. But this guy seemed like . . . such a bro, barely older than me, or so it seemed. The kind of guy I could see myself hanging out with under different circumstances. I tried to force my focus and listen to him, but all I could manage was staring at his lips curling slowly like rolling waves. *Holy shit man, I must be high.*

"Nicholas? I'm Doctor Perez. I see you had quite the scare." Dr. Perez motioned to the empty cups that sat on the tray next to me. "Did this help?"

I nodded slowly. I felt my legs melt into the pad beneath me. "Good," he went on. "We're just waiting for your blood work and urine sample to come back. In the meantime, I gave you a good dose of Ativan that will help you relax a little so we can figure out what's going on."

He sure did. Warm tingles rained over my forehead, and my muscles began to loosen like untying knotted shoelaces. It felt impossibly good, like sweet relief after the torture I'd endured in the past several months. Ah, the warm embrace of happy pills.

Yep. I was certainly high. Really, really high.

When Dr. Perez reappeared at my bedside, he went over my chart, and we covered a lengthy list of questions that he quickly ticked off with his pen as we scrolled down a column of yeses and nos.

"Well, Nick . . . what you just had was one mack daddy anxiety attack. It definitely had you out for the count, huh? Have you ever had an anxiety attack like that before?"

"Nah, man, first one," I slurred. That was a lie. A more accurate answer was that I was almost certain I'd had mini versions of this over the past couple of years. As if he was reading my mind, Dr. Perez continued.

"Anxiety attacks are brought on by mental or emotional stress and can range in intensity. Some feel mild or can include something I call 'air hunger' when you can't get a deep breath or begin hyperventilating. Others feel like actual heart attacks."

He nodded at me, looking concerned.

If I hadn't been so high, I would have nodded back. Everything he was saying rang ten bells of truth within, but the meds seemed to just steer me into space, and I settled on blankly staring straight up at the ceiling

"Also . . ." Dr. Perez paused in a way that felt hanging and imminent. "Your urine sample and blood work just came back. How long has your urine been the color of Coca-Cola?"

I took me a second to think back.

"I guess now that I think about it, it was dark yesterday and even darker this morning, like tea, but I just thought I was dehydrated."

"You are not just dehydrated, Nick. You have rhabdomyolysis."

"I've never heard of anything like that." He was making up some big word to sound smart.

"We call it rhabdo for short." Okay, fine. Maybe he's serious.

"What is it?" I asked.

"Rhabdo is a syndrome. Basically, your muscle fibers die off because of very intense and stressful exercise, which can over-load your kidneys to the point that they're unable to eliminate waste properly. Have you been hitting it pretty hard lately?"

"You know it! Swimming, sprinting, weights . . . you name it." I generalized, but the truth was maybe I really had been pushing myself a little too hard in the name of mental disci-pline and fitness, just like I did back in high school. That run a few weeks back had me utterly addicted to discovering how far I could push myself, and in a way, it was fun to play with the limit. I noticed my cousin Ben's signature phrase in my head when I pushed myself the hardest: "I don't give a shit." Any time I felt my body push back, my brain responded with zero tolerance. "I don't give a shit" became ever-present in my men-tal background. I wondered if I'd always said that to myself in the face of challenge, or if it was just Ben's way of keeping me strong from above with a little secret message.

"Yep, that's exactly how it happens. Now, this can potential-ly be fatal, but from your test results, it looks like we caught it in time. You're lucky, man—like really lucky."

My stomach dropped at the weight of the news. My nurse worked around Dr. Perez, preparing something on a tray be-side me before swabbing the back of my wrist to insert my IV drip. I stared up at Dr. Perez from my stretcher. He stood tall above me, his fingers hanging loosely in the front pockets of his scrubs.

"We're going to give you an IV that's going to help your kid-neys eliminate waste. And I'm going to keep you for an over-night stay so we can keep an eye on you. I'll be back in shortly, but Ana is going to take care of you right now, okay?"

The IV drip sat lodged inside my vein all night; an order for an overnight stay for monitoring lay on the table by my bed. As the sun tucked behind the trees and the sky out the window went dark, the contrast of the blinding lights inside my hospital room filled me with a loneliness that I couldn't describe. I closed my eyes and pictured myself all alone inside a clear vessel shooting through outer space: me as Major Tom, far above the earth. Nothing but the vast, expansive darkness surrounded me as I flew at light speed toward nothing.

The next morning, I woke to the warmest image: my mother sitting in the chair next to me reading.

"Mom!" The word burped out of my mouth in a muffled morning voice.

"Hi, baby. God, I'm so glad you're okay." She rose abruptly at my waking. "They called me the second they got the results, and I booked the first flight out."

"I left my phone in my dorm yesterday. My brain is so foggy."

Her auburn hair fell in a frame around her fair skin as she put her book away. Her deep-set eyes and full smile beamed at me like sunshine in that prison of a hospital bed. This felt like true medicine. We shared a deep sigh of relief between us. Thank God she was here. As a grown-ass man, I hated to admit it, but I needed my mom. Here I was, an almost twenty-year-old midshipman in the Naval Academy, and I still needed my mom.

When Dr. Perez appeared again, he was more informal, and he did a lot less nodding. He took my vitals while he made conversation with Mom and me.

"Your heart rate was high when you came in, but everything else checked out as normal. What's been going on that brought about so much stress?"

I closed my eyes and tried to scan my memories before answering. "Family drama . . . just a lot of family drama." My eyes drifted to the ceiling again, and I smeared the words into the air in the cool, bare room. The truth was I was still goddamn angry with my mom. So much truth I'd withheld from her over the years since we found out. I had bottled it all up inside me, and now it was bubbling over. I just couldn't keep it down anymore.

Dr. Perez went on. This time, I disliked each word he said more than the one before.

"I spoke with your guidance counselor at the academy." He paused. I wasn't sure if he was pausing for effect or grappling with how the rest of the statement would go. "We wanted to present an option for you."

When something bad happens in the military, being presented with an "option" means a higher-up knows your case and has made a call on it already. An "option" meant I could choose between two different predetermined flavors of *fucked*. I was pissing myself, and if I could have physically forced my eyes to widen, I would have. The best I could do was focus lazily on his hairy knuckles as he continued.

"We think a brief stay with us to do additional psych evals and provide support wouldn't hurt at this point. They have extraordinary guidance and doctors, and I feel that someone with your potential and grades would benefit greatly from that environment. Although the academy is extremely strict about disqualifying folks with mental disorders, they don't want to lose you, Nicholas. We can tell that you're one of the best and that you can bounce back with the right support. You just need to establish a strong base, and we can help you do that."

It could have been the Ativan, but any resistance that I normally would have had to such a dramatic phrase like "disqualifying" evaporated just like the anxiety, and the goofy words "do what ya need, my guy" tumbled out of my mouth with ease.

"Hey man, I'll get a nurse to wheel you down after lunch. We'll get a bag with your stuff to you as soon as possible." Dr. Perez patted the end of the bed twice before twisting around on one foot and disappearing down the hall.

At lunchtime, Mom wheeled me to the cafeteria. She sat across from me with her khaki pants and her legs crossed under the table. A scoop of egg salad sat propped up in a bed of butter lettuce in front of her. "Hey, so I just got back from a trip with the girls yesterday morning. I think I told you. We went down south and rented an Airbnb on the beach. It was beautiful."

Mom had taken a girls' trip with her college friends every year since I could remember. The six of them met up in small, understated vacation spots for spa days, nice dinners, and shopping. She always brought us hoodies or t-shirts with the logo of the place where they stayed. This year it was Destin, FL. Mom is one of those women who has lifelong, close friends. That kind of loyalty is second nature to her, which made it all the worse to witness such betrayal from Dad.

"I'm such a dumbass," I said in the lowest tone. A veil of shame draped over me as I processed aloud. "I just overdid it. I guess I just fucked myself up trying to escape what I felt." For the first time since my hospital adventure started, I felt my face get wet.

"Nick?" She placed a hand over one of mine. "I could say the same. There were so many signs along the way for me too. I bet those little ho bags wondered why I hadn't caught on to something in such plain sight. I should have known when your cello teacher warned me about the doctors with the boats, lake houses, and private planes and how I should be careful not to let my family get too close to those types because they all cheat. Who knew she was talking about Dad and Akapian and Parker." She was stronger recalling this out loud than I remembered, but the weight of how that torture changed her was heavy in her eyes. She still had on her smile, but there was a youthfulness about it that had disappeared. Still, the days of Mom sobbing on the floor in the middle of the night seemed to be a distant memory now.

She went on. "Or how about that time we were driving to Grandma's for Thanksgiving a couple years back, and I got that text. Do you remember?"

Oh, I remembered! It still surprises me how Mom kept it together while those women taunted her in their sly (and not so sly) ways.

"I definitely remember!" How could I forget? "We were about four hours in on the I-40 for Thanksgiving. What did the text from that girl say?" We both knew what the text said, but it felt like we needed to just say it out loud. I felt a bond strengthen between us as we recapped the drama.

"'Cat Fight.' It said, 'Cat Fight,' Mom." I remember Mom having just gotten a text about a quarter of the way into our trip to see Grandma. Luke and John Paul were zoned out in the backseat. She briefly looked down, then handed me her phone and asked me to read what it said. A text from a new number with a GIF of two little girls fighting and pulling each other's hair. The caption said "Cat Fight." *Disgusting.*

"That's right. That was Amber, another woman messing around in Dad's never-ending sphere of fuckery. I never would have guessed. She was always the understated, mousy little thing at Dad's office." Mom made a breathy puttering noise with her lips as she exhaled. "I never would have guessed it was her. Why would she send that, other than just to cause trouble? Nick, I truly saw evil when I saw those women trying to get a mother of three out of the way just so they could get a doctor, acting like *they* were the victims. I have never seen evil like that in my life." I saw the emotion inside her rise again like a slow simmer.

"You went nuts, and we had to pull over at that disgusting truck stop." I shook my head, but I couldn't stop myself from smiling. "We got out to get snacks and use the bathroom, but you didn't want us to be inside by ourselves with all the truckers. I watched you pace outside without any shoes, texting her back, then walking inside and getting in line with us so we wouldn't be alone. You had tears rolling down your face while we waited for the cashier to ring us up, but you looked so pissed."

"I don't know how I got so upset that I forgot to put on my shoes," my mom said, now cackling. *This* was how we dealt with things. She finished laughing, and her smile went away. "I just paced, Nick. I did a lot of pacing then. I should have had a keener eye for things like this. I should never have let it get to that point. I should have known he wouldn't stop after I found out or confronted him. I harbored so much hope, Nick. Thought he would change now that he'd seen the damage he'd done." She shook her head with a smile, and a tear, in the nostalgic remnants of disbelief.

"Even after my infidelity recovery group or couples therapy with that therapist who didn't know shit and found herself googly-eyed for Dad. I should have known way before any of this!"

"It was Erika, Molly, Skye, Taylor, Amber, Erica . . . another one spelled another way. Man, he really covered his bases, didn't he? And those were just the ones I knew about. Am I missing some?" She paused for a moment, took a long, deep breath, and sat back in her chair. This time I put my hand on Mom's to calm her. She was getting frantic and mad, flooding, instead of depressed, and I knew that she could get really, really loud soon. I hoped she didn't.

I sat across from her as she unraveled the facts of our family falling apart. A rich, warm goop of sadness dripped over both of us. Just being able to say their names out loud felt somehow freeing. This backtracking, making sense of nonsense, connecting all the dots. This was facing my anxiety head-on . . . with her. The tense charge in our conversation lifted, and Mom's face softened. I broke our gaze and stared down at the table. The egg salad still perched politely in place, waiting for her to take a bite. Mom smiled at me, still with tears, and I did my best to smile back. We let the memories fade back into the past where they belonged.

I could feel my body still holding onto this massive amount of anxiety. My stomach seemed to buzz with unease. Mom was right, of course, when she said I wasn't supposed to be this stoked in the middle of plebe year. It was hella tough. I also wasn't supposed to be in that state of mind—stressed out, panicked, so emotionally exhausted that I was not only being admitted to the Walter Reed but for a *psych* eval. How did I end up here?

* * *

After lunch, I gulped down another dose of administered Ativan for my anxiety and let my eyelids sink down to a close when the gentle rattle of a wheelchair opening startled me awake again, and the same nurse, Ana from before, stood inside my curtain, instructing me to transition into the chair. As she helped me down and into the seat, I took another deep breath. It just felt right . . . weird, but right.

Now that I was stable and being transferred for psych evals, at the insistence of the Navy Chaplain, Mom headed home, giving it to God and the professionals. We hugged goodbye as she saw me off. We promised to talk tonight on the phone once I got settled.

Ana pushed me along the blinding fluorescent hallway and into an oversized elevator where we parked right beside a stretcher carrying an older man. My nurse pressed #1 as he slowly craned his wrinkled head to look at me.

"What are you in for?" I blurted out courageously, feeling the need to make conversation because this dude was just staring at me.

"Heart surgery tomorrow morning. You?" The old man's face was weathered, but he had a powerful look in his eyes, the kind that told me he probably could have beat the shit out of me when he was younger.

I took in another breath as our elevator landed on the ground floor. As the doors stretched open and we began to push forward, I craned my neck to keep eye contact and replied, "Same." This Ativan stuff was wild.

We strolled under a skyway, through automatic double doors, and down a long corridor where a woman stood waiting for me in front of a sign that read "Walter Reed Psychiatric Ward."

"I'll take him from here," she said to the nurse with a wink. "Hi Nicholas, I'm Amy. I'm the chaplain here in the ward. Let's get you checked in, yeah? Dr. Perez let me know you were headed this way."

"Sounds good," I replied. My words sounded gooey and stuck to the roof of my mouth like disintegrating bubble gum. I both loved and hated those two little white pills.

As she wheeled me into the ward, Amy made conversation. "Nicholas, I've gone over your list of emergency contacts from the school. I'll go ahead and get you checked in. Would you like to make a call to family members who need to know you're here? I know your mom was here and just left, but I just wanted to double-check." She was holding a clipboard that I knew had those items on it, and she seemed wildly uppity for some reason. Maybe she drank too much coffee.

"Nah," I said with a sigh.

"Okay, well, when you're ready to use the phone, this is the designated phone." She pointed to a red rotary phone that sat boldly on a desk. It looked exactly like the one my grandmother had in her old farmhouse we used to visit as kids. I loved the way the wheel swooshed back in the other direction after each rotation.

I let her push me past the hallway of doors. 105, 106, 107 . . . I leaned my head back and watched the fluorescent lights pass above me until we came to a stop at 109.

"This is you." Amy leaned over me and grinned warmly.

"This is me," I answered.

2

PEAKS AND VALLEYS

I remember that it was a cool Monday evening—a soothing reprieve from the damp August heat that dragged us all down. The sun hung low in an orange-and-pink marmalade glaze washing over the trees. Through the front window, our neighbor's dad shuffled groceries from their SUV into the house. The streetlights flickered on, illuminating the autumn tones in the air. How simple it all seemed then.

Mom was making my favorite dinner. The pungent odor of blue cheese opened up as I leaned over, watching her slender fingers dig into the crumbling, blueish veins that stunk in the best way. As the oldest, I loved to help Mom cook. It was something we had done together since I stood bolstered on my little stool and made messes with Christmas cookies and banana puddings. Now I was sixteen.

I've helped her make this particular dinner probably ten times over the past few years. They were my grandma's recipes originally, and Mom "made them more modern," she always says: three-cheese potatoes au gratin, roasted herb chicken with beets and carrots, and a classic wedge salad.

Mom, Dad, John Paul, and I made our way to the table carrying dishes, while Luke continued to bounce a ball in a three-point wall/floor/glove triangulation. It was an ever-present background soundtrack we'd all grown to tolerate (and even love) over the years. As I passed by with a platter of stacked salad wedges, the worn scent of Luke's leather glove coated the air. We sat down to observe the first eyeful. Luke didn't miss a beat, and no one said a word. This was the obsessive side of my brother. We knew he'd join us eventually. He was probably just counting and needed to complete a round perfectly before he could walk away. It was a version of Luke we'd all (except Dad) learned to accept by now.

Dad was always a little repulsed and upset if we all did not immediately do as he said, and no matter what wonderful food Mom made, he would find a way to find fault with something put on his table. He turned his nose up at the cholesterol content of every little thing, mumbling under his breath while gesturing with his hands at his prepared plate as if he was judging the poor potatoes. He and Luke wouldn't touch the wedge salad, while JP and I always asked for seconds. Lucy skimmed the floor under our feet and then paused, hopefully waiting for our "drop du jour." Dad sipped a glass of red wine, while Mom looked around to make sure all of us boys were taken care of. We were. We always were. Sometimes I wish she'd stop serving us and pay attention to her own plate.

"Lucas, stop with the ball and come sit down," Dad announced to Luke who paused for a few beats, ignored the invitation, then continued with his triangulation repetition. We'd made it a habit a while back to do something called "peak and valley" at family dinner, sharing one point in our day that was the highest and one point that was the lowest.

This was the one time in the week where I got any sense of who my dad was or what he was doing lately. I could never really figure Dad out. A doctor who had made a name for himself in the past couple of years, he definitely had a confidence about him that I admired; or maybe it was his rich Spanish accent. Either way, there was just something about him that was always a mystery. He spent most of his time entrenched in work-related things: trips, philanthropy, and community service events, at the office or in surgery. He'd all but disconnected completely from us in the past couple of years, almost as if he'd checked out of the family. I rolled my eyes at the thought.

"So, my 'peak' was that I asked Paige to go to Homecoming with me, and she said yes."

As the youngest of us brothers, JP laid it out. "She's your girlfriend."

Mom's eyebrows hoisted up her forehead, and she grinned. Dad said nothing while he sliced into a piece of chicken.

I continued. "My 'valley' was that Mr. Lutz announced that SAT prep got pushed up by a week, so we're all scrambling now."

Mom nodded to Luke who was still hyper-focused on creating the perfect baseball harmony with the floor and wall. Out of the corner of my eye, I could see Dad peer over at Luke with disdain.

"My peak," Luke chimed in, as if feeling both Mom and Dad's eyes on him. "I found out that we play St. Matthews this weekend. We're guaranteed to kill 'em!"

"Lucas!" Dad shouted, startling us. He always reprimanded us without making eye contact.

"And your valley is that you smell like shit?" I blurted out. I couldn't help myself; it was true. Luke was a dynamite baseball player, obsessed even. I could see him going pro someday, but, heavily into sports and in the thick of puberty, the kid smelled like rotten, curdled milk mixed with B.O. Even though Luke was two years younger, you could tell that he was destined to be a super handsome man: with thick dark wavy hair, deep brown eyes, already chiseled features, he had a good six inches on me and was built like pro wrestler. He'd come home and complain about the kids at school calling him "Andre the Giant," but secretly I envied his looks and stature. He could practically crack the bat in two and kill a homerun like it was nothing. He was just a freak.

"Luke, put the damn ball away and SIT DOWN," Dad barked

again. We collectively let the tension dissipate with our silence and the delicate clatter of our silverware against our plates as Luke sat down.

"Let's try again," Mom said to Luke once he had sat down and after a few moments had passed.

"Peak: St. Matthews. Valley: Apparently I smell!"

Mom let out a hearty giggle, giving the rest of us permission to do the same. I took a perfect bite.

From my view, I could still see Luke fiddling with his worn baseball under the table. I silently peered up at Dad. He couldn't see the ball from where he sat, but we could all tell Luke was looking at something just below eye level from the table. I braced for impact.

Dad boomed. The resounding bass of his deeply accented voice stunned us. His chair squealed as he shoved back from the table and threw his napkin down. I could feel the hot anger in the reverberation of his footsteps through our hardwood floors as he raged over to Luke. As Dad took my brother by the arm with force, Luke threw his ball across the kitchen in a panic.

"Three times!" Dad bellowed as he yanked Luke's arm up the stairs. Had it not been terrifying, it would have been an almost comical scene, being that Luke practically matched Dad in height and weight. Dad slammed Luke's bedroom door behind, a standard indication that Luke would be there for the rest of the night.

John Paul and I helped Mom clear the table that night. I didn't see Dad again until Thursday. I never knew why, but I had my ideas.

3

BRECKENRIDGE

The year before, we took a family ski trip. As kids, we learned to ski at those fancy, rich people ski resorts where parents could dump off their kids and then relax on their own terms. We learned to ski in herds of anxious little heirs on powdery kiddie slopes. Mom and Dad eventually bought a house in that ski town, but early on we stayed at that French ski-in/ski-out resort, with their buttery French food and their red-faced host with his equally buttery accent. The cozy town was lined with humble inns with fireplaces exhaling picturesque plumes from chimneys in the distance. The cobblestone streets were perfectly dusted with fresh snow as we muddled along to dinner as a family.

That night, making our way back to the resort early from dinner, JP's altitude sickness was getting worse by the hour. Having only sipped water at the table, he now was feeling the onset of vertigo, so he and Mom went up to the room while Dad, Luke, and I stayed down in the lodge. As a high school kid, I studied the hotel restaurant crowd. My eyes were drawn to the older guys I looked up to and wanted to be like one day. We always were mixed up for dinner, and I always made an effort to sit with the fanciest looking people. I met a lot of extremely interesting people that way. Investment bankers, nuclear engineers who worked on secret projects, resort owners. I felt most at home with them.

A roused group of preppy college boys on winter break hovered on one side of the bar with three snow bunnies in training. Their peacoat collars popped high over their monogrammed button-downs and cocky attitudes. I studied their posturing from across the lodge while I waited for Luke to come back with a pizza he'd charged to the room. Dad ordered scotch on the rocks and made small talk with a tall woman next to him. Country music spilled in from the other room and bounced off the exposed wooden beams while Luke and I scorched our mouths as we scarfed down a white garlic pie with barbecued shrimp faster than I would have liked.

Lovers wandered in and out, sipping warm mugs of winter libations. Two twin girls dressed identically in their après-ski apparel played tag in the lobby while parents socialized. Two pink pompoms atop their woven winter hats bobbed behind oversized leather chairs, ducking in and out of goose down–stuffed couches. A roaring fire in the lobby flickered warm amber ambiance along the textured walls and reflected in a hallway of giant floor-to-ceiling windows. I decided to take a stroll and check out the night-skiers while Luke stayed to see if the bartender could turn the channel to the Ohio football game.

I couldn't help but notice how picturesque it all was. Tiny black ants inching down the lit tree-peppered slope in the distance. In the foreground, the perfect view of a long, thin illuminated pool and its vapor spreading into the navy night sky.

Suddenly, my gaze was pulled away. An image moved out of the corner of my eye, and I shifted slightly to see. I could vaguely make out the edges of a man and a woman interlocked, kissing. A row of snow-dusted foliage stood between us. The outline of her head thrown back laughing as the man wrapped his arms around her torso bearing a gregarious grin. *This place is the shit*, I thought to myself. As soon as I thought it, as if perfectly orchestrated, they turned slowly to the massive double doors. Her brown knee-high boots scattered powdered snow as she pranced away, their fingers finally losing contact as he reached to keep her by his side. Her shadow swept into the light through the windows. The woman at the bar, and . . . *Dad.*

A wash of panic rolled over my shoulders and draped over my chest and back in a paralyzing prickle. I stood curiously still as I watched him watch her disappear through the lobby. A strange smile lingered on his cheeks. I'd never seen that particular expression on his face before. I let him slowly float back in and rejoin what was now a small crowd around the flat screen TV that played the Ohio game. I forced my body to move out of this hypnotic shock, walking slowly and without aim until I found myself opening the door to our room.

JP lay slumped over in a heap on the far corner bed. Mom knelt down, picking up ski attire that had been thoughtlessly strewn around our suite from earlier in the day. I watched her until she noticed me standing there. "Hey, honey," she cooed in her raspy, Southern accent. I loved how even her voice sounded old-fashioned, warm, and worked.

"Hi," I managed, still not moving.

She continued to busy herself around. "You okay?" she asked, noticing something was off with me.

"Dad was with a woman," I sputtered in the most undercover way I could muster. She continued to tidy uninterrupted. I wondered if she even heard me. I pushed the haunting memory to the very back little corner of my brain until it began to bleed out of me again without my control. "Like another woman. Kissing." JP began to stir in bed, and her attention was redirected almost willingly. I didn't push it any further. That was the night I learned the meaning of denial.

From:< mom >
To:< navalkid >

Nick—

What we have gone through is quite extraordinary. If I could have made it different for you, I would have. I would have made it different for all of us. But today you did the bravest thing. You made the choice to get the support you need to heal and learn how to handle the heavy things that life sometimes throws at us. I feel like this stay might be God's way of helping you through this. You know, sometimes He delivers what you truly need through some of the darkest times. I'm so sorry that was your dad. I'm hurting with you.

P.S. I called Beth and the family to tell her what's going on, in case they can help out being so close.

—Mom

4

GRAVITY

My next night in the hospital, Amy showed me to my room. I don't know what I expected, but this was certainly not it. Maybe I'd been reminiscing too much about being back home. But here in this new room, I took a deep breath and took it in with a slow spin. Any notions of privacy that I might have had were quickly sucked out of me with one glance around. A stark white room surrounded me. A bare, rectangular mattress sat, nestled in the kind of generic twin frame you see on furniture commercials or staged in fake dorm rooms in college brochures. It was not lost on me that the jarring reality of how sparse this room was seemed to match the emptiness inside of me.

As I turned to assess this new setup, somehow it was noticing that glass square centered at the top of my door that brought it all home. All at once I saw it: this wasn't some overnight stay in a hospital. This wasn't me moving into the dorms at college, or a weekend vacation in a hotel. Suddenly, a different kind of weight anchored me to the ground. I was in the psych unit. For the first time in my life, it's like it truly hit me: this was what gravity felt like.

"Well," Amy jolted my attention back into the present. "What do you think?" she said. She was way more enthusiastic than I was prepared for. I'm not sure if it was the shock of my new surroundings or the stress of the day, but my eyes met hers with electricity that stunned me. Soft green eyes stared back at me. She was younger than I first caught onto, and tall. Evidently, the meds were still working their hypnotic magic because after seeing how pretty she was, all I could manage was a half-smile and a slow nod.

"I see the meds are still in your system. A good night's sleep will do you good, Nicholas. The nurse on call is on the way to get you settled. He'll be just another minute," she said. She hit me with that sweetness again.

Before I knew it, another body stood in front of me. An older skinny white man in the same hospital green scrubs as Dr. Perez began asking more boring questions that seemed to go down his mental checklist. Amy came in with a duffle bag that my roommate had packed for me. The nurse rooted through my belongings, scanning for anything dangerous. He set aside my psych unit–approved essentials and toiletries and dropped the remainder of my contents in a ziplock bag. Everything in the entire place was suicide-proof, designed to make sure no one could take that final step off the ledge. Even the toothbrush was made out of this outrageously flimsy material that could never be made to harm.

"Are you scared I'm going to make a shank out of my toothbrush or something? I promise, I'm not suicidal . . . or violent."

He just stared up at me expressionless. "We do it for everyone in this unit, man, it's not personal," he said in a dismissive tone.

Efficiently, he emptied out the contents and quickly disposed of the plastic baggie in a large black trash bag he'd brought along, proving he was no amateur. He dropped a stiffly pressed stack of bedding on my mattress, wished me well, and turned to leave, presumably so I could settle in. I gave him a raised eyebrow and then looked myself over as he stared at me. His eyes suddenly widened, realizing I was still recovering from rhabdo and needed some assistance, as I started to lean and strain under my own weight.

"Hey man, I'm gonna need a shoulder to lean on real soon or I'm gonna fall." We both chuckled, and he helped me to sit in my room's chair before he got to work making my bed. When he was finished perfecting his "tight corners," he folded a fluffy duvet at the end. It reminded me of home and how Mom made our beds.

Even though it was simpler than my dorm room at the academy, there was something refreshing about having my own space for a little while. The last thing I remember, I was shoving the corners of my pillow in its case before I lay down to take a break. I can't remember a time I was this downright exhausted. Consciousness seeped out of me as I felt the last moments of my heavy limbs sink into the mattress.

I woke up with the sun blaring in my eyes through a tiny crack in the window shades. A quarter-inch slit of blazing, bright truth streamed in perfectly at my eyeline. How could something so illuminating also be so aggressive, so blinding? I pulled the stiff pillow over my face. The cover was stark white, coarse, and medical. *Aren't pillows supposed to be soft and warm, tender and malleable?* "Holy hell," I grumbled. "This pillow is trash!" I whispered in my morning rasp. A wave of nausea overwhelmed me as my pulse throbbed in reverberated hiccups. This definitely wasn't a dream.

I sat up in bed, my feet teasing the cool tile floor beneath me. Reality made itself known once again, like a heavy layer of scum bobbing in my belly. This was real.

I peered at the clock. That couldn't be right. I had slept fourteen hours? Breakfast was in twenty-eight minutes, and the idea of eating rubbery sausage links and viscous, monochromatic, prepackaged scrambled eggs triggered my gag reflex. I scurried to the toilet as I felt my stomach hurl upward, hoisting up hints of yesterday's lunch with a side of sour bile.

Minutes later, I pulled myself together and headed out to the cafeteria. A wheelchair had been folded up and collapsed against the wall for my convenience. Thank God, because I still needed a little help. I was now no stranger to the nausea that anxiety caused for me. All I knew was that I was sick of feeling sick and ready to make a change. *What else was I going to do with that time?* I thought to myself as I entered the room that smelled like frozen meat and Brussels sprouts.

"Can I sit here?" I half asked a rotund man in his mid-sixties. He said his name was "Phil" as I pulled up the table and dropped my tray down on the smooth cream-colored linoleum cafeteria table. Phil's swollen diabetic calves hung lazily in his wheelchair leg prop. I couldn't help studying the bursting sores flanked by scabby, wax-like scales. My chest convulsed with a shiver, as goose bumps washed down my forearms in microscopic pings.

"I'm Nick," I muttered in a low tone.

Phil looked like a genuine lunatic. His physical appearance was summarized by his eyes, which seemed wild and hyperactive as they shot around in his skull, yet simultaneously lifeless. He was deeply unnerving, and it was hard for me to imagine how he might have once been a chief. All of the patients here had military backgrounds. Their issues ranged from PTSD to generalized anxiety disorders to addiction. I had a hunch that Phil had witnessed some kind of the carnage, the war-brand of crazy. He seemed to have truly lost his sanity.

He was the same man from last night. I had wandered past a crack in the door—evidently, where I'd be meeting in a therapy circle. A sheet of paper taped to the door read, "Therapy Circle in session . . . Shhhhhhh!" He sat hovered over his wide-legged posture, shuffling a stack of playing cards aggressively. I witnessed him sounding off to another man who sat across from him, shuffling and venting, shuffling and venting. He was apparently arguing loudly with the nurse about the crappy menu, but he was way angrier than what would make sense for complaining about shitty eggs. His impulsive outbursts were definitely born of deep trauma. Phil's rants reminded me of Mom when she was at her lowest points.

My stomach and I quickly decided to have a WWE ladder match again. Every single thing rubbed on me like the metallic scuff of a silver sponge, and just existing today had my body feel road-rashed like after a terrible accident. My physical self was an emotional wreck, and it was time for me to clean up the carnage.

I can see it now: my body ejected, as metal crunches and bodies violently smash into steering wheels and glass shatters against skulls. There was that call from Erika's husband . . . the flash of a red traffic light, wafts of scorched rubber creeping into my nasal cavity. Then reality hits. My gag reflex again triggered movement in my stomach in this freezing cold room. My imagination can be dark and catastrophic sometimes even to the point of becoming physically ill these days. I only use willpower to keep myself from throwing up.

I took a bite of scrambled eggs and then another. I felt them land in my stomach, and as the nuisance of my own nausea faded, Phil opened his mouth again—this time to talk.

"Why so dead in the eyes, son?" he asked. I looked up from the scrambled mound of yellow fluff on my tray to instantly lock eyes with a middle-aged black woman from two tables away. Her gaze on me wasn't threatening or creepy, but instead was strangely comforting. I let her watch me while I answered Phil.

"Oh man!" I shook my head in reflection. "I think I'm just in shock. Never thought I'd be here, I guess." Phil raised one eyebrow with a smirk. I saw for the first time that, in his eyes, there was a real person desperately trying to hold on.

That morning, I sat in our first of two daily therapy share circles, my tailbone grinding against the hard plastic chair through my sweatpants, having finally been able to leave my wheelchair behind. I felt more like a petulant child than a grown man healing through personal family trauma. There is truly nothing more humbling than rewinding back to square one. Like a kindergartener, I was learning how to take turns at speaking when I almost seemed to vibrate with anxiousness. My knee started doing that up-and-down thing again.

I could feel that woman's gaze on me again out of the corner of my eye—that woman from the cafeteria. Her right knee bobbed with energy just like mine. I couldn't tell if I was unconsciously copying her or she was copying me. Eight of us sat in the circle, and even though she didn't join us, somehow it was still as if she was right here. Still, she sat four rows away, anchoring the very last seat on the far right with a mainline view directly on me. Anyone else in the room staring at me the way she stared at me would have been a mortal threat, but her vibe was soft and wholesome, like a warm chocolate-chip cookie. But like Phil, she had a look in her eyes that made her seem half dead. I realized I really didn't want to talk today. But that wasn't an option for me while I was here.

I let myself be pulled into a trance as I watched Phil shuffle his pile of playing cards in that same violent manner. Dr. Ruben nodded to me, and I slowly gazed upward.

"Guys, this is Nick. He's a new patient here. Let's all welcome him." Dr. Ruben sounded like he'd recited this opener hundreds of times before.

A collective "Welcome, Nick" scattered in the circle.

I saw the black woman shift in her chair from across the room. She leaned in as I allowed the discomfort within to overflow. She wanted more from me. I looked around. I saw all eight bodies leaning in, waiting for me to say something. Their attention felt better than I could have expected, and I felt my stress and anxiety transform into a type of hunger that I had a hard time putting words to.

"Honestly, I felt better before I came in here. I was sick to my stomach this morning. Now I'm just pissed at the shitty eggs." Our group of nutcases laughed, and Phil dropped back in his chair, like he was feeling vindicated after his earlier outburst. He managed to shoot me a smile.

It really was a shitty joke, but our band was so desperate for humor, for the ability to take themselves less seriously, that they made me feel like Jay Leno, even while I sat in my uncomfortable plastic chair, wearing a medical smock and looking like a moron.

Dr. Ruben calmed down our giggles with a silent hand gesture. He stifled a smile while he fought to say his professional spiel. "I can see that we're starting to get acclimated already, Nick. I just want to remind everyone to try and help Nick out and ensure he feels welcome, as we always do whenever we have a new member."

* * *

After a week in Walter Reed, with my daily morning circle with my fellow lunatics, I was finally feeling better. Walking, moving, and feeling like my normal self. At one of our group meetings, I finally felt safe enough to share. So, when all eyes turned to me to open up, it felt like my words flowed like someone had turned on a faucet.

After nearly twenty minutes of incoherent rambling, I found myself saying, "I'm just a grown kid with daddy issues. What can I say?" My right leg bobbed again with a furious heat as laughter fluttered amongst the other patients.

"Can you say more?" Dr. Ruben asked. This time, I couldn't *not* say more, and the truth began to spill over.

"A while back, I found out that my dad was cheating on my mom, but I don't even see it that way. The way I see it, Dad cheated on 'us,' the family. He cheated on us all. My brothers were spared a little, but being the oldest and being so close to Mom, I took it the hardest. I always had a sixth sense with her. I could always tell when something was going on. When she was laid out on the floor, or the weeks after my dad moved out . . . They never divorced, but she couldn't stand for him to be in the house after that. I'd wake up to her screaming in the middle of the night. 'Whores! Those whores!' she'd scream over and over like a track. I would spy on her from a crack in my bedroom door from across the hall. Sometimes she'd see me and tell me how sorry she was, and I'd hear her breathe behind her door while she sobbed. Other times she'd smash items around her bedroom. Sometimes they'd break, and sometimes it just made a mess. It was always cleaned up by morning. But why is it always the women who get blamed? My dad could have stopped them. He didn't! He didn't stop them. He had sex with all of those women . . . so many women. So while Mom was chauffeuring us boys around and taking us to baseball games and those stupid Suzuki method violin lessons and cooking and cleaning and keeping the family running like a machine . . ." I shook my head vigorously in disbelief. "And the worst part is that he's totally dismissive of it."

My voice welled up with power and volume in a way that triggered an urge to clench my jaw down in rage. "I ask him. All he says is, 'It's all rumors and gossip. Just rumors and gossip.' But I know the truth. It's like . . . torn us all to pieces." I stifled the prick of tears and held my breath to control whatever this swelling thing was inside. Thank God we moved on. No one wanted to touch that one with a ten-foot pole.

"Have you ever said that out loud before?" Dr. Ruben transmitted calmly.

"Nope," I whispered with shame, as tears began to stream from the corners of my eyes without control. I felt weak, breaking down in the midst of these strangers, but even before I completed that feeling, Dr. Ruben interjected.

"Well, Nicholas. You know that healing happens *in* connection, not alone in your own head. In order to heal, you must give up the secrets. You are in a safe place to express these thoughts. Simply saying them out loud to the group is very powerful. Exposing our secrets is a great way to create more freedom in our lives. In a way, those secrets lose their potency when you state them out loud. They begin to hurt less and less. Do whatever you need to do, but get them from the inside out."

Tears continued to stream down my face as my body followed his instruction. His voice was clear and mellow like the surface of water, and his words felt cool to the touch. My thoughts felt like a swirling tornado, barely able to identify what was hurling past in pure chaos. But I held it together while Dr. Ruben brought our circle to a close. A part of me thought I was dying to keep whatever this ghost was inside for so long without becoming The Hulk. And maybe I was dying. Maybe that's why I was here. Why I *needed* to be here. I let that thought go.

We were dismissed for "Activity." With a choice between a hike and yoga, I chose a hike. More opportunity to stomp out this monster within. Damn, it felt like it was growing outside of my control. I hustled to my room, shoved my feet into my running shoes, and jogged back to our meeting spot at the front, just beyond the automatic doors. But I wasn't alone.

My legs squirmed with excess. I needed to move now, and I'd be damned if I was going to let anyone here slow me down. I'd had enough of that.

From:< mom >
To:< navalkid >
Subject: How's Your First Day? (Sorry about all the "whore" talk)

Nick—

When your dad and I first met, we were in the trance of love. Your father could look at me from across the room and my body temperature would skyrocket. He used to cook for me and I for him—we filled each other's hearts and tummies. Geez that sounds cheesy, anyways, I don't remember when it first started to go south. Perhaps it was while my career was bustling in D.C. (it wasn't easy being an attorney and a mom in those days). Maybe it was before the move, but maybe afterward. I can't tell anymore these days.

I'm not sure of anything anymore. I used to know who I was, what I wanted, how to get there . . . I know nothing now. MaryEllen is taking me to see a doctor tomorrow. I honestly don't know what I'd do without her. She says this woman is someone who deals with situations like ours almost exclusively, with women like me. That gives me hope, but I still feel so disoriented and, quite frankly, embarrassed. I simply couldn't hold myself together. I imagine many women, many mothers, do it better than I did.

I remember getting a text about one of your dad's affairs—while I was picking up your little brother from school. I lost it, Nick. I dropped JP off at home and drove as fast as I could to Dad's office. He was in the parking lot carrying a big tray of leftover sandwiches from the flirty pharmaceutical rep's visit earlier in the day. What a sight: turkey and ham sandwiches all over the parking lot, on the "whores'" cars. Nick, I'll never forget it . . . mayo and mustard smeared all over. That one approached me with her high and mighty, sassy attitude, and something deep inside of me just knew she was one of them. I couldn't control my temper. The sight of it . . . their nice respectable cars, slices of bread falling to the pavement, and they just stared at me as I screamed and threw more sandwiches. They just stared.

I really lost it, didn't I? And you had to witness all of my crazy. I'm so sorry, honey.

Really, the only one who had any heart was Darlene, who's been there since before we ever moved to town. She always did cut through all the bullshit small talk. Not like those other whores.

It's all so different now.

A new purpose, and you boys are all gone except JP. It feels lonely here all on my own, but I might just be strong enough to recreate my life while you're recreating yours.

—Mom

5

SHOCK AND AWE

"How ya feeling, Lord?" Colonel Manchester hollered back as I struggled to keep up with him. Hearing him now on the trail, Manchester came off as a badass to me. With a good thirty years on me, he was twice as fast. The man was a machine. As I willed my muscles to accelerate, that now familiar creeping anxiety expanded in a throbbing wave inside. I felt it grow. And as I remembered how this feeling magically transformed into a sort of untapped power in therapy circle, I quickly remembered how I got there. I was beginning to see it as power instead of anxiety, and I wanted to use it for good this time. All this time, it was just untapped power. A warm laugh echoed inside my chest at the realization.

"What'd you call me?" I called out in a harmless but curiously menacing way.

"I called you *Lord*!" he repeated, louder this time. The word *Lord* tumbled down through the branches in echoes.

What the fuck? Why was he calling me that? "Hanging in. You?" I mustered between breaths.

"Well, easy does it. You don't want to overdo it again."

But I pondered. *Why the hell would he call me Lord?* Like Jesus? Like God? Like British royalty? It began to rub at me in five ways, all in the wrong direction. My attention pulled down to my legs as memories of therapy circle—or TC, as I was starting to think of it—reemerged. The power swelled inside my quads, and I wanted to explode into a full sprint, but I held back. Something about the colonel engaging with me fought hard for my attention.

35

"Eh, anything's better than where I been, kid." His breaths were as steady as a train.

I gave it a minute to answer. I was still ruminating on why he called me *Lord* or even the fact that he gave nicknames to mere strangers. "What do you mean? I mean, I know you've seen some stuff but . . . life is pain, man. You gotta learn to manage that shit or you'll die." I left space for him to fill it. Manchester was wise. He wasn't just a patient but a man who was in a long-term outpatient recovery program here at the hospital. His insight was endless, and I'd just met him.

I felt the mountain under my feet press back against me with a test. I pushed back. I had never appreciated an incline like that in my life. This unforgiving slope forced our charged confrontation to dissipate with necessary intermittent silences to catch our breath. Maybe he wasn't quite the machine as he first presented. As I gained on the colonel, neither one of us wanted to admit it, but this hike was turning into a competition. It was kicking both our asses. Between our heavy, huffing exhales, our phrases grew shorter and shorter in labored pants. The two of us found a way to keep a cadence in our words that felt quite soothing and safely predictable.

"Well, we have a lot in common." Something lonely grew out of him. His voice got softer as the words unfolded in between desperate breaths. My curiosity was piqued. That dark hunger woke up again, and my body begged me to dig in a little deeper . . . not only into the conversation with the colonel, but into this mass of energy that seemed to just be getting bigger within; maybe into this mountain that pushed against my body with such resistance, but most definitely into his beckoning tone. I knew something was there for me, and I waited patiently for it. I could feel it coming. "Nick, I'm pretty much your dad in your story. I was the cheater."

My legs found a pause, and as my pulse pulled tight against

my throat, I felt that familiar restriction of rage spiral from the crown of my head, in the muscles that squeezed into my eyeballs, down through my throat, wrapping in a thorny heat around my ribs. I had a choice—suffer in it as it turned to muck inside me, or . . . use it.

All at once my legs exploded in front of me. A blur of garbled green sped past my periphery. In eight seconds, Manchester was toast. I felt him try for me, but my body didn't care for courtesy or being the good kid anymore. I used my limitless stores of anxiety as fuel to just blast past him.

This was unfamiliar territory. I'd recently taken up running out of sheer discipline, being in the academy, but this felt very different. This felt like it was just for me. I surprised myself with an exhilarating speed that propelled me up that massive mountain, hurdling over fallen tree trunks, swooping around sharp turns and in and out of tight nooks that suddenly posed zero threat. Familiar faces whizzed by. I felt superhuman, and I seemed to only accelerate for what felt like half an hour. And as I forced my speeding legs to come into a downshift, a new breed of pride arose in me.

I'd always tried to ignore these inconvenient eruptions of emotion—cramming them down, turning my head the other way, pretending they didn't exist, hoping they'd just go away. But the past couple of days in here were doing something strange to my insides. I began to wonder if those old tactics of ignoring really ever work. I had a sudden urge to face this. I had to finish my conversation with the colonel.

★ ★ ★

After lunch, I headed to the community room for quiet time with some of the other patients. As I passed the double doors at the entrance looking down the hall, I nearly tripped on the right wheel of an old Coast Guard officer whose chair was being wheeled in by the reception desk. The sight of his sickly state gave me a chill. I looked the other way.

All of the sudden, I began to notice just how good I had it compared to the other patients here. Long-term or permanent trauma, debilitating PTSD, addiction, and personality disorders were all in front of me. Of course, there were others with milder cases like me, but the stark contrast was blinding.

A week earlier, Mom had shared a Facebook post from another plebe's mom. This girl was in my third period and was diagnosed shortly after the school year began with a possibly terminal heart condition. She had a life vest defibrillator and was confined to a wheelchair within a matter of hours. Picturing her signing the discharge papers that slashed her dreams at the jugular must have taken more courage than I had.

No doubt, training to be an officer was an extraordinary feat, and plebes had it especially hard. Daily hours of intense interval training and intense emotional pressure; rigorous and exhausting standards proved detrimental to some of us. It was all to weed out the weak ones. The US Naval Academy was for the top 1 percent, not just some average Joes. Plebes were cut left and right, dropping like flies in that first year. So far, I was one of the 1 percent (fingers crossed).

As I entered the room and took inventory, I looked up and saw HGTV proudly being displayed on our lowly TV where it must have hung for the past twenty years. We weren't house-hunting or landscaping our backyards or updating our old kitchens, but one day in the ward, I had just switched the channel to HGTV and watched episodes the entire day with Chief Drea. HGTV was so much better to watch than the mind-numbing garbage that the nurses put on, like the local news station, Discovery, or the E! channel. HGTV from then on became pretty much the official channel of our mental ward, with Chief Drea and

I as its sturmtruppen. Sometimes we would come out of our rooms to a gentle argument as the rest of the patients begged someone watching *The Avengers* to turn it back to HGTV, and Chief and I would harangue the person and the nurses until our sacred channel once again graced the TV. It was dumb, but in the ward, it was the funniest thing of all time. We even recruited other henchmen to enforce HGTV's 24/7 dominance of the TV, and after a while, the only people who attempted to watch something else were the new patients. One time, a big spectacled army specialist ironically called us "a bunch of nuts" when we went ballistic after he tried to watch *Avengers: Age of Ultron.*

I craned my head around to see four sets of eyes peering up, glued to HGTV. Andrea (or "Chief Drea," she bluntly reminded me) and I caught eyes, and as if she could read my thoughts, she raised her arms straight in the air and said, in a complete monotone, "HGTVVVVVVV!" Her big brown eyes slowly rolled back up to the screen as her right leg continued bouncing furiously. Those who dissented to HGTV were outnumbered by lunatics. There was something really therapeutic about keeping that channel on: it gave us an excuse to act like a bunch of goons, and it gave us a little fake and harmless drama every day as we fought to keep it on at all times.

Four of us sat on the thirty-year-old pilled plaid couch. Phil, Chief Drea, Colonel Manchester, and me . . . we seemed to have established our permanent spots since the night before, from most to least crazy. A good hour into *House Hunters International*, I took a deep breath and . . . OMG! I took a deep breath. It had been months of having "air hunger," as Dr. Lopez had coined it. Suddenly, I found myself freakishly undisturbed for a moment as I sat on this ancient couch with these damaged strangers, in this cold, square room. But as weird as it all was, there was an inner fabric that bound us all together like patchwork. I was beginning to realize an underlying similarity in all of us. I just couldn't quite put my finger on exactly what it was yet.

Last night, we sat around a table like knights at Arthur's roundtable, discussing mock government. Dr. Ruben suggested we form some sort of alliance outside of TC so that we could "practice our communication skills in a democratic way." "Skills for the real world," he called it. Evidently, they'd tried this concept before. I learned the hard way that the roles were still up for debate, and, as usual, Phil had to make a scene.

"I don't wanna be fuckin' president, let me sleep!" he offered in his pounding Texan accent as he scratched yet another sore on the back of his left hand. I always looked at Phil and wondered if they'd put dog cones on his hands or something so he'd stop picking at himself.

I loved to study Phil in his outrageous scene-making. He fascinated me. Phil had a good heart, but he wasn't exactly a man you could trust. He'd turn on you in an instant.

"Phil, you don't do the *job* of president anyways." I watched Phil hold his breath and turn a deeper shade of purple, as he glared at Chief Drea, who continued to drop truth. "You can't just yell at us and then go hide in your room, *ya schmuck*." Drea and Phil's arguments were really just coarse humor between two salty chiefs. We always just sat and watched the show.

"Well, hell, then! How about we have *Lord Emperor* here handle being president." Evidently, they'd collectively decided on this alias without my consent. He nodded in my direction. ". . . see how good *he* does . . . little golden boy!" A sprinkling snicker bounced across the room, followed by a silence that felt like agreement. I finally realized they were calling me that because of my silver-spoon academy background. We had kind of a reputation in the fleet for being a bit aristocratic.

"Hey, if I'm already a Lord Emperor, why not add President to my title," I stated confidently. And with that, I became President

Lord Emperor of the psych ward patientry. It just made it even easier to keep HGTV on.

* * *

That night, Titus, the maintenance man, asked me to help lift a corner of the "divan" so he could mop underneath. The dingy-white coiled strands sloshed in a worn yellow bucket by his feet, while the fumes of bleach swirled in an expanding cloud in the air. How funny. Grandma used the word "divan" instead of couch. Instantly, memories of playing in her old country house filled my mind. I hadn't really thought of her since I saw Mom last.

I raised one side of the divan for Titus. Instantly, the smell of bleach disappeared. I closed my eyes. I could feel Grandma's house again. The soft wafts of homemade bread filled each room like warm clouds. She would have a loaf freshly sliced into these thick pieces with pats of fresh chilled butter on the side. My brothers and I would devour a whole loaf in five minutes.

I remembered that kitchen still so vividly. Dark wood cupboards, a farmhouse sink that Mom had pictures of us boys bathing in as babies. The framed Bible passages strewn around on walls, quotes of family, and an old-fashioned furnace that I'd burned my fingers on more than once as a kid. The memories were still in me. I could feel my grandma with me.

"Nicholas?" My eyes flashed open, thwarted out of my memory coma by a nurse ducking her head in. "Phone call for ya," she whispered, noticing I was having a moment. Titus gave a nod, and I set my side down, sprinting to the phone.

Plopping down next to that old red rotary phone, I picked up the receiver.

"Hello . . . "

"Hi, Nicholas!"

It was Dad.

41

From:< navalkid >

To:< mom >

Mom—

I saw this old Coast Guardsman wheeled into the ward today. He must have been six foot ten with these long gangly legs and his shoulders hoisted over his hollow belly. He wasn't well—almost catatonic. I'm not sure what happened to him because he's in another section, but there was a way he reminded me of you that day you got the call. It's like he was somewhere else, not here. I'll never forget that look in your eyes that day. It must have been January because I remember our Christmas wreath still on the front door when you slowly let it float open and just sort of wandered outside for a while without a reason, the phone hanging in your hand. That man just talking and talking into the air while you wandered out into the street.

I heard a couple years after that Garrett's dad had been cheating on his mom too. Actually, it was much more than just hearing about it. After practice one night, Garrett and I went to grab a quick dinner. We passed by that motel over by the old field near DeWitt Highway, the one where Luke used to play baseball at when he was super little. Remember? Garrett saw his dad's car, which isn't hard to spot. So we parked across the street in a lot and watched him like spies. I remember my heart racing! So scared we were going to get caught. We had just picked up Sonic, and I remember spilling chili on my shirt when I looked up and saw the motel door open and Garrett's dad walk out with some woman. NOT his mom. I can tell you that. I think there were four of them that came out of the room, but we ducked behind the dashboard and I didn't see others, just shadows. Wait, didn't Garrett's dad and Dad work together? So weird. Is this whole town cheating, or what?

Anyways, the numbness is starting to wear off. Honestly, all I feel is anger now, erupting from deep in my belly. If anger could sting, it stings. Everything irritates every last inch of skin on my body. An older man helped me through some of it today. His name is Colonel Manchester. For once, someone in here gets my humor. Somehow, he arrived at calling me "Lord Emperor" because a fancy academy kid is supposed to be running this place. I don't actually feel like I should be running this place, everything just seems so strange, but at least now I can breathe and I'm learning how to cope with this.

—*Nick*

6

CABIN PRESSURE

As nighttime set in, it always felt like there was a drop in cabin pressure in the psych unit. On airplanes, I'd observed the flight attendants at the front of the plane with their pleasant smirks and pointing fingers, while they read their safety scripts into the handheld CB, the springy cord bouncing in the background. I'd wonder what it would feel like to have the stale air sucked out of this flying capsule that had promised an unscathed delivery of loved ones across whole continents. The shock, terror, carnage.

After more than a week in here, it was all starting to feel eerily similar to being thirty thousand feet up in the air. A hundred-plus strangers, trapped in the same experience; we were all in this together, no matter the outcome of our recovery—our futures unknown. I guess it could be confused with the feeling of falling in love. More accurately, it was the feeling of allowing the uncomfortable sensations of this process to take their shape in our lives. It was a loss of control in a way. We were helpless victims of the physics of healing.

After hearing Dad's voice that night, I physically experienced the air being sucked out of me with one fell swoop. The moment I hung up that familiar red receiver, everything went silent inside. A deafening ring in my ears lingered as I sat teetering on the arm of the hallway lounge. For the first time, I could hear everything he wasn't saying, everything he was holding back, the running stream of lies. I had never had the awareness before, but after a handful of therapy circles, private sessions with Dr. Ruben, and focusing on recovering from this . . . *thing*, I was beginning to notice behaviors I never had before.

I know he called to check in and show me he cares about me, but Dad plays a cheap game. Conversations with him were like watching rocks skip across the surface of a lake—quick, just skimming the surface enough to create that feeble radial wake, and then disappearing like it was never even there. I suddenly noticed all the ways he skirted around facts by providing delightful generalizations all wrapped up shiny and pretty, like on Christmas morning. Deflecting seemed to be a third language to him—a man of great skill in shining the light in the other direction, but never truly on himself, and finally I got it—Dad was manipulative and charming! Suddenly it became quite clear how he could have led a secret life, or six, or ten. The jury was still out on how many affairs he actually did have. All I know is that it was enough to wreck my life, not to mention my mom's and brothers'.

* * *

After our call that night, I scuttled down the stark white hallway and knocked on Manchester's door. I needed a grown-ass man's perspective. I needed to hear his story if I was going to make any sense of my father's bad behavior. I knocked three times with the back of my pointer finger, then heard him shuffle toward the door on the other side.

"Lord President Emperor!" His weathered face greeted me.

"Manchester. Hey, man. Wanted to see if you had a minute. Kinda tryin' to work some things out. I wanted to see if we could finish our conversation on the trail the other day." His joking tone disappeared instantly. I'd thought about how this conversation would go quite a few times. After stressing too much about it and still not having a solid plan, I decided to wing it and trust that I wouldn't mess this up. It was just a conversation after all. I had had those before.

"Sure. Let me, uh, put on some shoes," he said as he pulled the door ajar and retreated to grab his sneakers.

As he reemerged and closed the door behind him, a waft of Irish Spring came along with him. We walked side by side, gaining permission for entry to the courtyard at the front desk, then going out through the automatic double doors. We strolled. I caught another zing of his soap. It reminded me of Dad. Dad used that regular green bar of Irish Spring with the creamy white swirls in it. I knew that wasn't where the similarities ended. The silence was getting uncomfortable. I knew I'd have to say something soon, but Manchester was so cool. He just let me take my time until I was ready. I took a deep breath.

"On our run the other day . . . you said something about how you were my dad in my story. Manchester, I'm working through some big stuff with my father right now, and there are some things I know I can't discuss with him. Honesty isn't really his strong suit. I want to know your story." I paused. A cold chill washed over my shoulder blades. I held my breath as we both stared at our feet stepping almost in unison.

"Stuff like that isn't supposed to be easy," he exhaled.

A buzz zagged through the air between us like lightning. Manchester pressed his lips together in thought as he nodded his head, compiling his next sentence. Out of the corner of my eye I caught a familiar shadow of a rhythmic movement—Chief Drea's leg. She sat slumped over on a lonely bench with her forearms resting on her bobbing legs, this time with a man at her side. They wore wedding rings. He stroked her hand softly and sang a bare version of "Love and Happiness" with a light-hearted tenor, whistling the horn solos. Drea's right knee was still going a million miles an hour. She noticed my attention on her and turned to catch me watching them with her bulging brown eyes—something desperate but unreachable stared back at me. I began to get curious about her story too.

"So I haven't spoken to my son in thirteen years," Manchester admitted boldly as my focus fell back on him.

There it was again. The cool, easy breeze of a feeling that was always between us. Talking to him was easier than it was to talk to my own dad. Two birds chirped, hidden in the lush green trees that surrounded us, and before I knew it, Manchester was casually saying words like "attempted suicide" and "rehab," and at least one other "divorce" hung in the air. Words like that only served as a complement to the bleak afterglow of the sun, which had just tucked itself in for the night.

"I didn't know how to tell my wife without wrecking my children too. I knew if I told her I was fucking around with other women, I'd lose everything. I'd lose her and everything I loved. She was a boss too—the boss lady of our house, that's for sure. Denial became my best friend. I would wake up every morning, press the reset button on my life, pretend that I was all the best things about myself and that none of the despicable things I'd done ever existed."

A heavy summer vapor surrounded us as we both came to a slow stop to face one another. Manchester's ice-blue eyes, drenched in remorse, allowed something to soften inside me. As tears dripped from the corner of his eyes, a bead of sweat fell from my hairline.

"I just learned to live a life of denial . . . for years I lived like that. Lies built on more lies built on more lies. I managed to build a whole other life out of lies, kid. Until one day . . . God, it's so cliché." I could see a flush of shame in his cheeks.

"One day, at work. It was my secretary, actually, who walked in and caught us. I'll never forget the moment. I felt like such a big shot. I was leaning over her chair, and I had my hands in places they should not have been. I had been sleeping with,

I mean, I fell in love with her . . . this woman." Manchester looked loosely down at his feet as he continued.

"She was my client, and I absolutely had betrayed my wife in a thousand different ways with her. There were many other women too, but she was the one who did me in. To tell you the truth, I am disgusted with myself. But I did, in fact, care deeply for this woman. I still do. Anyway, my secretary and my wife had become good friends over the years, so naturally I was toast that day . . . that was that."

Manchester had my undivided attention. This was sounding a whole lot like what I knew about my dad.

"That was your wife's *D-Day*," I said with confidence, remembering Mom.

"My what?" Manchester looked up to make eye contact with me, with tears in his eyes, before understanding the term on his own. "Discovery Day," he said with resolve. A deep whimper erupted out of his chest as the corners of his mouth sank down with a weight.

A wrinkled furrow made shapes between his eyebrows as I felt my own memories quickly coming to the surface.

7

D-DAY

On June 6, 1944, American troops invaded German-occupied France in the largest seaborne invasion in history, known as D-Day. The invasion began the liberation of Nazi-run Europe. Seventy-two years later, there was another D-Day: one that would expose secrets and bring the dark truth to light.

I barged into my bedroom on a mission. Lucy, curled at the end of my bed like an oversized croissant, jolted out of her mid-afternoon nap, as I flew in looking for my cello. Out of the blue, the phone rang. *That's weird*, I thought. Our landline almost never rings. Then it stopped. I grabbed my cello leaning against the corner of my bedroom and started to head out when the phone rang again. On the second ring, I picked up the receiver on my bedside table, but before I could say hello, I heard Mom already talking to someone . . . a man . . . a very upset man. I held still and listened carefully.

"I think you know Erika," the man stated in a hostile tone. "Evidently, everyone knows Erika!" His words lingered as Mom attempted a few different sentences, only to restart and try again.

"I'm confused," Mom said outright. "Is this about my mother?"

My grandma had slowly been losing it for a while now. First, they called it dementia. That was when she still knew us by name. Farm-raised and strong, Grandma had a way of cracking up our whole family with her unfiltered comments. So, as her disease began to worsen, we all found the truths that came out of her mouth extremely funny.

One Sunday, a few months ago, after Mass, we all went as

a family to visit Grandma in assisted living. She'd just been to the beauty shop and her hair was perfectly curled, picked, and sprayed just the way she liked it, but her face told another story. Even though her heart was all there, something was amiss about her—a distance of sorts. I'll never forget this moment where, mid-sentence with Mom, Grandma turns around to Dad, who was standing behind Mom watching the TV overhead, and blurts out, "Victor! You're a son of a bitch. You know that? Just a son of a bitch." The five of us stood stunned in a pause before breaking into collective laughter. I thought she was a lunatic then, but now I think Grandma saw the truth about Dad long before Mom did.

Grandma always gave it to people straight, but along the way our family had made a phrase out of her blunt delivery, which the rest of the women in our family evidently inherited. "Going full Margaret" was a term we used when a woman gave her unbridled opinion to someone else. No one could do it like Grandma.

She was truly one of a kind. Grandma was kind-hearted and generous—the quintessential grandmother, with a sense of bold humor that provoked open-minded men to ask her for life advice. She was a no-bullshit, tell-it-like-it-is kind of woman, and as she got older, her give-no-fucks attitude was in full bloom. She'd made it a ritual to have a drink at a local pub once a week. Except that Grandma didn't drink besides her one weekly O'Doul's, and the bar didn't sell nonalcoholic beer. Over the months, Grandma made friends with a group of middle-aged gentlemen who invited her to join them as their in-house source of wisdom, and before she knew it, the bartender started carrying O'Doul's just for Grandma. She just had the type of power as a woman that made everyone orbit around her, especially men.

But those were her good golden years. It wasn't long before her doctors officially labeled her unfiltered truths as Alzheimer's and she took a turn for the worse, which had Mom on high alert. It had become a third job for Mom . . . always keeping an eye on Grandma's progress . . . or lack of progress. I think it took a lot out of her to come to grips with the truth that Grandma was never getting better, and we eventually lost my grandmother on Easter Sunday 2012. I reigned in my reminiscing and pulled myself back to the receiver, which I had pressed too tightly to my ear.

"No! This is Erika's husband. Erika's my wife. She's been screwing your husband for months now." Erika's husband continued to rattle on, his strong Southern accent making his words feel even stronger.

I didn't move. My brain couldn't comprehend what was happening. I needed to let the pieces land so they could fit into something I could comprehend. Suddenly, memories of that night in Breckenridge bubbled up effortlessly. I hadn't just imagined it. I stiffened, listening for the next clue that I could even remotely place.

"I'm sorry. I think you might have the wrong number!" Mom affirmed. Mom's words came out in jabs as she attempted to make sense of the call.

"I'm sure I have the right number, ma'am. Is this Maggie?" the man tried again.

"Yes . . ." Mom replied, barely breathing.

A long pause spread between them. I pressed the mute button on my end but kept the receiver close to my ear. I tiptoed out of my room and to the top of the stairs. I could hear Mom rustling around in the kitchen. I froze, waiting for more.

"My wife is Erika," he went on. "She's a nurse at your husband's office. I've seen you outside in your yard. You seem like a nice lady. I didn't have the guts to go through with what I wanted to do to him before, but I have to tell you that your husband has been with my wife. They are having an affair."

In an instant, a thud echoed up the stairway and I sprung to action. Scurrying down the stairs and whipping around the corner of the kitchen, I witnessed my mother in a heap on the floor with the phone at her side. Erika's husband was still rattling off details, which sounded mostly like gibberish. Fragmented details sputtered out of him: "Friday," "middle of the night," and "hotel on DeWitt Street."

"Mom!" I knelt down beside her, my school khakis wrinkled from the day, a mustard stain on my right thigh from lunch. She was still breathing and just barely fluttering her eyes open again when the man on the other end of the line began a trail of details again. I took the phone from my mother's hands and listened closely, still piecing the story together.

The man sounded scattered, panicked, and almost manic, as he choked back silent tears from a distance. Mom stood up in a stupor and took the phone back out of my hands, as the man continued gabbing.

"I'm sure you have the wrong number. My husband is not like that. We have a family. Victor would never do something like that."

My mom spoke in breathless whimpers as the truth began to dawn on her. I could hear the man from the receiver as I leaned in toward Mom. The man went on.

"They all go to this lake house. I have pictures of them out on your husband's boat. There is a group of them that go. Your husband goes with them and that toad from the office."

"Toad?" she repeated.

"Yeah. I call him 'The Toad' because he actually looks like a toad. He's some Egyptian doctor, but he's as sleazy as the other ones." Mom laughed with one exhale as her eyes stayed fixed to one spot on the wall, taking it all in. Mom covered the receiver with her hand and pulled it away from her mouth as she whispered to me.

"I know exactly who he's talking about. He DOES look like a toad! It's Doctor Afara with that weird mole under his right eye." Both of our eyes widened in disbelief. I knew exactly who she was talking about. I'd seen that toad-looking doctor at Dad's office. It felt as if a veil had been pulled back and a whole other world was being revealed to us . . . the real world. This was the truth about Dad and his colleagues.

The man continued. "I downloaded that tracker on her phone, and it traced her to a lake house instead of the hotel she said she was staying at for work, so I began to dig."

I could see the wheels in Mom's brain turning, making sense of and piecing together the random information into factual truth. And like a lead blanket, it hit her. I will never forget the look in her eye. In that moment, Mom changed.

"Call MaryEllen NOW!" Mom commanded, pulling herself up to her knees.

I rustled through Mom's purse that hung lifelessly on the kitchen counter, pulled her cell phone out and dialed. No answer. I texted.

My fingers flew across the screen. "MaryEllen, it's an emergency. Please get here ASAP!"

And with a swoop, "OTW!" appeared in the text bubble on Mom's cell phone screen.

Within what seemed like thirty seconds, we both heard a squeal around the corner. Craning my head out the front window, I saw a black Escalade screech to a halt. MaryEllen flung open the door without closing it and sprinted up our stairs into the house in a huff.

MaryEllen lived two blocks away in a house that Mom always secretly envied. They had become close friends over the years, first through us boys and all our sports. Mom was always laughing at MaryEllen's undercover agent abilities. She was always the go-to when needing information on someone.

Eventually, Mom gifted MaryEllen with the affectionate name "Supersleuth." Over the years, they'd gained each other's loyalty and trust and shared a very specific type of humor that I certainly didn't get but admired.

"Let me take it," she offered to Mom, as the phone dangled lifelessly in Mom's hands. Not having a clue what was happening, MaryEllen immediately took charge. She was like that: able to jump in with no experience and take the proverbial bull by the horns. Taking Mom's cell from me and the home phone from Mom, she listened intently, gathering more information from the distraught man on the other end of the line as she began to search Mom's cell.

"I came to your house to kill him," I heard the man say as I leaned in toward the earpiece that MaryEllen was holding. "I waited outside on the street, in my truck with a gun, but he never came home. I just watched you and your kids come home from school, getting groceries out of the car, hauling it all in. You seem like a nice lady. I just don't want to hurt my wife. I don't want to hurt her. Don't hurt her. I don't want to hurt her."

I looked to Mom. The blood had drained from her face. Mom had experienced a drop in cabin pressure in that moment. And as she shuffled out the front door in a dense daze, I watched our lives change forever.

★ ★ ★

My room was at the end of a long hallway on the right. It was quiet down here and away from the commotion of visitors, family, and doctors bustling around and transitioning from midday shifts. It felt safe down here at the end of the hall.

That night in the ward, I shifted in my sheets. "Ward" was actually an overdramatic term for this section of the hospital. It was quite cozy for the most part, and as days here grew on me, the room that looked so bare and cold in the beginning now felt like a safe nest for my personal recovery.

Mom's D-Day was years ago. My, how things had changed! I shifted more. I shifted around until I was exhausted from shifting, then I shifted some more. My brain felt like it was on fire. My legs begged to be worked. My heart was chugging like a freight train. Revisiting these sad memories did something to me physically. Maybe this was all part of the process. Everyone says how we should leave the past in the past, let bygones be bygones, but I'm beginning to call bullshit on that old story. Dr. Ruben says that we can't truly heal if we don't go back and rectify our past. He said we have to do that to make sense of it, to untangle the things we don't understand.

Over the next few days, I spent every last minute of free time working out this furious war inside myself. The gym became my best friend, but this time I knew my limits.

From:< mom >
To:< navalkid >

Nick—

I remember that day well. Very well! It is tattooed in my memory, in fact. That day felt like my 9/11. You don't remember 9/11 because you were a baby, but it was the day everything changed for Americans . . . for the whole world, really. It is when we realized things weren't what they seemed to be. It was the day we learned that there are predators in real life, just like out in the wild. We all have this suspension of disbelief about life, about our own lives sometimes, where we want to stay naïve about how dangerous being alive really is. But that's not how Grandma raised me. She taught me to live fully and with fervor, and with compassion. Family has always come first with us, until that day. 9/11 was the day we all realized we were the prey. That's how I felt the day I got that call. I felt like prey to unseen predators.

Nicholas, I am so sorry. I am so sorry for your father's choices. I am sorry I couldn't change this for you or repair it more quickly or protect you from being hurt. You always say that I was never the same after the day I got the call. We both know it's true. Things like that change a person regardless of how we forgive, heal, and move forward. Our family will never be the same. You boys will never be the same. This shattered my idea of what I thought my friends and family and community were. SHATTERED. I've had to reinvent myself too, Nick. I lost everything. I can never get back that safe home I used to walk into and see you three boys running around in the backyard with Benjamin. Ben is gone too. Grandma's gone now.

But it's time to rebuild and recreate. I swear, there was something in the water in that town. With those people. That wasn't community—not the community I know. The community I know puts families first. They put honesty first. They protect each other. Without family, we have nothing, baby. Nothing. Family is the DNA of society. You're my DNA. It all starts again right here with us.

—Mom

8

URBAN MYTHS AND OTHER LIES

The weights dropped with a *whop* that vibrated through the soles of my shoes. We were allowed one workout per day in the psych ward, and to be honest, it was just what the doctor ordered. I finally felt like a champion again. I was feeling stronger, my endurance was slowly increasing again, and most importantly I felt like I'd mentally drawn a boundary with myself on what was actually physically healthy. Learning to "listen to my body" was actually very true shit. Should have done that all along, but we're never taught how important it is.

In my senior year of high school, cliché phrases of mental discipline were drilled into my brain by our track coach. It was "Mind over matter," "Your body does what the mind tells it to do," or "Pain is weakness leaving the body." Phrases like that always got my fire raging, and it felt amazing to still be able to dive headfirst into seeing how hard I could push my body. Even at the academy, my company leader would echo similar taglines like "Your mind will give out before your body does, sailor!" But I think he got it wrong. My mind was hell-bent on being the best. It was my body that was a little behind the game. This was the part that I needed to rewire.

My brothers and I were made for that kind of thing, though, especially Luke . . . even my cousin Ben. All of us boys in the family were machines. Ben was three years older than me, a brick house with quite a few extra pounds. And even though he was older, he always felt like a little brother to me in a way. He'd inherited Grandma's laissez-faire attitude and hilarious sensibilities.

As kids, we used to wrestle out on his front lawn. My uncle and Mom were siblings. They lived a more modest lifestyle in a neighborhood in another state, but his house always felt like home. Ben pinning me down in a series of suffocating headlocks forced a stronger boy out of me. Even as a kid, I remember this feeling inside, an ever-present competition between my body and brain, born in that strangling chokehold and Ben's shouts of "I'll put ya to sleep. I don't give a shit!"—a feral tagline that only he could pull off and still be loved. He was just real.

During my eighth-grade year, we drove to Ben's house for family lunch after Mass. He and my Uncle Joe had spent the past couple of months fixing up Ben's dream car. They found a way to completely rebuild a worn 1982 El Camino into a legitimate super sport. After almost a year of time-consuming renovations, it was far from the eyesore that it once was. This time it boasted a high-sheen silver paint with deep black racing stripes along the hood, steel wheels, and blue velvet seats; the quintessential white dice dangled over the rearview mirror: Ben's *El Chic Magnet* was complete.

As we pulled up to the house, his prized possession perched proudly in their driveway; Ben himself, the dude with the most unfuckable-with presence, waltzed to our car with a billowed chest. He came out to greet us on that sunny Sunday afternoon. There was a new confidence about him that day. I sensed a change in my rough-around-the-edges, blunt, straight-shooting cousin. Ben was becoming a man.

"A couple of months until you can drive her, huh?" I said, before Ben practically tackled me as I stepped out of our SUV, reminding me that maybe he wasn't actually becoming a man . . . yet.

"A few more weeks, man!" he gloated, guiding me to his new pride and joy. "It's like seeing God in person, right?"

We nodded to each other slowly as we examined the piece of art. Personally, I wasn't a fan of the El Camino, but as a kid just hitting puberty, I secretly envied his tenacity and follow-through. It took balls to drive a car like that.

That next Monday, Mom got a call. Some meth-head had stolen Ben's car out of the driveway in the middle of the night and taken one hell of a joyride.

"Smashed it right into a tree," Uncle Joe said before taking a lengthy pause. "Lots of trees, actually." The wrinkle between Mom's eyebrows became sad and serious, and her lips pulled into a tight frown like they do when she's overwhelmed with emotions. "Unbelievable! Two weeks before he turns sixteen," Uncle Joe spilled. "That idiot had to go and ruin it for my boy . . ." His voice trailed off, and I could tell through the phone that his mind had too.

A few months later, Luke, JP, and I piled in the backseat of our Suburban at the carpool line at school, hauling our backpacks and slinging stinky sports bags into the third row. Mom was eerily quiet. I knew something was wrong before she opened her mouth. I could always read her really well like that, like a sixth sense. In a strange series of unfortunate events, Mom had gotten another call from Uncle Joe, and this time the news made my stomach drop and heave like the dips and peaks of a rollercoaster. I felt my hot cafeteria lunch make its way back up my esophagus, but looked out the window at the trees zooming by to redirect the impulse.

Mom said softly, "They found a tumor in Ben's brain."

She was crazy about Ben. She always called him Benjamin because she thought it sounded angelic. She'd always treated him like one of us boys, like her own. She found his directness refreshing and honest. I could feel her heartbreak. The rest of our ride to Suzuki music lessons was cold and silent. I tried to work it out in my head. It took me another couple of days to start asking Mom more questions about what would happen to Ben.

One night before bed, I sat eating leftover blueberry muffins Mom made that morning while she sipped her tea.

"Can I call Ben?" I asked.

JP's head perked up from his homework, and we both stared at Mom.

"Uh, sure! I don't see why not. Should we try tomorrow?" It was her fake positive voice that I knew too well. JP and I looked at each other. I looked back at Mom.

"Mom, be honest with us."

She paused as she took a sip of jasmine tea and swallowed as she gathered her thoughts. I felt my heartbeat in my ears. Suddenly, my worst nightmare flashed in my brain: our family all standing around Ben's casket at his funeral. Surely it wasn't nearly as bad as I suspected. Then Mom gave it to us.

"Ben has a tumor in his brain. The doctors aren't optimistic."

She pressed her lips together the way she does when she feels sorry for someone. It was her silent apology for a moment that felt so hollow. My stomach sank, and I felt the heat that came with hearing truth cover my entire body. JP began to tear up as I reached over and pulled him into me.

"Ben?" JP sobbed into me.

"Yeah, buddy. But everything's going to be okay," I choked out as I felt tears fill my eyes. We both knew everything was not going to be okay.

Mom walked around to our side of the kitchen table and nuzzled us both into the sides of her stomach the way she did when we were little boys. Except this time, we were young men and I was deep in adolescence as a junior in high school. This was real life.

"Don't say anything to Luke tonight. I want to tell him myself tomorrow. Hey, maybe we can make a family trip to see Ben too, huh?"

A year later, on the most somber day I've ever known, my hand held his casket as a pallbearer at his funeral.

★ ★ ★

Another week of rewiring passed in rehab at the psych unit. I found myself falling into predictable patterns with the HGTV gang, and taking on the role of *president* while Phil scowled at me from across TC.

First it was Erika. I only knew about Erika because Erika's husband called on Mom's D-Day. But if I think back before that, there was Taylor and talk of Taylor. Then there was Skye and Skye staring at my brothers and Mom and I at the pool that one summer. There was the Lake House Orgy Office Gang (as I had affectionately labeled them in my head) with the private jet on so-called "work conferences." "Weekends at the lake." And it was a type of community service, all right. There was a lot of desire for the well-being of others and very generous donations going in and out of that place, forty-eight hours at a time.

Evidently, Dr. Brooks (at Dad's office) and his associates would take his private plane to his lake house mansion with the nurses and some of their friendly and very open-minded friends to have a free-for-all party. It's like he took it as a personal challenge to see just how little he could make me think of him. At this point, he made me sick when I thought of him.

Then there were the warnings from my music teacher at the Suzuki school that I overheard by accident. Come to think of it, I learned all of this *by accident*. I still can't recall how I found out about all the women, but it always seemed to come through a third-party, word-of-mouth type of thing, but never from Dad. Dad always denied and deflected. Terms like *denial* and *deflection* I'd learned here in rehab. I always thought rehab implied substance abuse, but I'm starting to think we all need some sort of rehabilitation from life as it happens. There was most definitely something in the water here in this tiny town of wealthy doctors and the nurses who served them, and Mom, my brothers, and I were smack-dab in the middle.

It was as if there was some illusive underground sex community that only existed as an urban myth. I mean, I'd seen these women. I'd seen them at Dad's office while I dropped something off or ran errands. These women were not the kind of women cast in famous movies about infidelity. These women were not Mena Suvari in *American Beauty*, or famous, cool muses like Glenn Close in *Fatal Attraction*. They weren't even close to the hot, iconic nurse archetypes, like that fantasy every guy has of the low-maintenance girl-next-door sorority chick showing up at a Halloween party, but underneath you know they're the average cool girl and you'll see her in Calculus on Monday morning. No!

These women were the ones you see in the toilet paper aisle at Target with a kid in the cart and baby hanging off their chest in a sling. These women were like the regular teachers at my high school, like the woman who did the paperwork at the DMV when I got my license. They were the ones you passed in the mall parking lot in their Honda Civics. These women were normal, mousy, and unassuming. But they were fucking Dad. This urban myth was true.

9

THE DARK HORSE

I remember Mom in her messy stage. Those days after Mom's D-Day were a vast landscape of sadness and anger. Mom changed that day. Something inside of her died or was born, depending on how you want to look at it.

One day after school, I heard rustling around in Mom's room. I broke from my geometry homework and tiptoed around the upstairs railing. I gave a slight knock before opening her bedroom door.

"Mom?" I whispered.

As I stood in the doorway studying her, Mom, her back to me, stood on her balcony, peering off in a daze. With the double doors swung wide open, random men's clothes were strewn around the room in a trail behind her. Sweaters and jeans dangled over the railing.

"Mom?" I inquired more loudly. She spun around in surprise, as if she'd forgotten anyone was home. With mascara smeared and tears running down her pale cheeks, she looked into my eyes and said nothing. I looked around the room and into the closet.

"Dad's clothes?" I said with a new brand of pride. After all, I was angry at him too.

It was like every cliché movie I'd ever seen about a woman being cheated on: a distraught wife flooded with a cocktail of emotions desperately flings open the upstairs balcony doors and proceeds to throw out the contents of her unfaithful husband's closet. It was a desperate plea to rectify the injustice, to feel some sort of relief from the unbearable torture of betrayal, from her shattered family.

But in that split second, I really saw Mom. Not as my mother, but as a broken-hearted woman doing her best to make sense of the world being so unfair. Those movies existed because moments like these really existed. This was real pain, real grief, real . . . life. Mom was having her real movie moment.

She took thirty more seconds to fully break down in a deeply powerful sob that forced her to her knees, and forced me to do the same. Then, all at once, the storm calmed. She took a deep breath, wiped her eyes, and walked down the stairs quietly. As we passed Gloria, our housekeeper, at the bottom of the staircase, she joined us without words, and the three of us walked out to retrieve Dad's clothes from the lawn. Mom and Gloria spent the next two days doing his laundry to reassemble his closet to completion while he was "away on business."

* * *

With my discharge coming up, Mom decided to come visit. We decided to go to a meditation class the next morning—a class I had attended a couple of times before and was now getting the hang of. As I tried to get comfortable in my "easy cross-legged pose" with my sit bones firmly grounded beneath me, a soft hand touched my shoulder. I craned up to see Amy beckoning me into her office with a gentle toss of her head. I hauled myself up and followed her across the fluorescent hall and into what felt like a cave.

Her office was a dimly lit square room with a heavy mahogany desk and a white, tufted leather armchair that propped up my backside. I instantly felt more confident as I lowered myself in. The deep tan walls were clad with Christian stained-glass art and famous Bible passages. An oversized vanilla Yankee candle burned robustly on the corner beside the black velvet back of a picture that framed a shaggy Saint Bernard with droopy jaws.

Amy was a tall, lean white woman with the build of a life-long runner. She wore a pair of grey slacks and a loose t-shirt with a simple black blazer that hugged into her waist. I remember the first day I was admitted. She was the one who greeted me. Peaceful warmth practically emanated off her skin. The softness in her eyes begged for me to tell her all my secrets, and somehow she reminded me of the women in my family that I loved. She had Mom's intellect and solidarity. She felt understated and smart, strong. I could trust her.

She sunk down into her big leather office chair and stared cleanly into my eyes with an omniscient grin. The reason why I was in her office was unknown, but I wasn't hating that I was here. I knew Amy always came with love. I suddenly felt another distraction loom over me: a distraction that couldn't hurt me so badly. One that was healthier. One that could actually help inspire me here in rehab. She did save my life, after all. And even if I would never admit it to anyone else, I admitted to myself that I had a massive crush on Amy.

10

THAT'S RIGHT
(YOU'RE NOT FROM TEXAS)

"You've got quite a fire about you, Nick!" I felt Amy's warm words reach me in little waves that rippled out in honesty. "You had us all on edge there for a minute, but we're very happy to have you back. And it's actually perfect timing." Her eyes widened bright with positive energy. "I'd like to discuss the possibility of your time here coming to an end and what that might be like for you."

Right then, I heard a light knock on the door. Mom stood in the doorway.

"Can I join you?" Mom said with trepidation.

"Of course! I'm sorry," Amy said. "You were deep in meditation and I didn't want to pull you both out of it, but it's better that you're here. We can all reconvene together now."

As I sat across from this pillar of a woman, Mom seated at my left, this felt like an exit interview of sorts. I felt like I was getting fired from the pysch unit, but something told me this was a good thing.

"I know it's been an uphill battle, these past few months and years, Nick. I know your story by now." Amy's eyes softened as she pulled Mom into the conversation. Amy had a way of looping people in with her energy. I'd seen it as she cofacilitated therapy circles over my stay here. She could magically draw someone's attention by taking a breath, by slowing her speech, by merely blinking. Amy was one of those women who didn't have to try. She had a soft power about her that made you want to be your best when you were around her. She was hypnotizing in a way.

"Well . . . it's been a heavy week, so I'm just trying to take this all in stride. You know, Amy, a lot has happened that has led up to Nick's stay here. A lot of . . . trauma. I know you are aware of some of it."

Mom always got emotional when she talked about this stuff in the past. I felt my breaths begin to get more and more shallow as I anticipated more intensity from her. I was still very angry with her. As much trauma as there was, Mom could have handled Dad's infidelity escapades logically and saved herself (and us kids) a monster amount of stress. The key was what Dr. Ruben taught me, and that's empathy for another person's experience. I may have not done it like Mom, but I'm also not in her shoes, and she was handling three heartbreaks . . . not just one. It makes sense that the way she reacted wasn't logical. In her defense, she really did marry a case study.

"In the past couple of years, we have lost my mother to Alzheimer's and his cousin to a brain tumor. Nick has seen the collapse of our family because of his father's infidelity, and I'm a mother who is definitely a different version of herself. Nick has had a nervous breakdown and a life-threatening illness—some really serious stuff. A few of these things are just life, but it was the cheating that really did us in. Not just me, but Nick and his little brothers too."

A bubble of charged tension bobbed in the room as Mom took a breath.

"I'm a traditional person," she continued. "I care deeply about our community, and the nucleus of community is family. Family is the DNA of society, Amy. I guess I see community like a sort of safety net. Like when things go wrong or get tough, community should be there to pick up the slack, take care of those who are suffering, and support the structure of family. Of course, my close friends and family were there for us, but for the most part, everyone was very tight-lipped. That disturbed me." The fact that those nurses and doctors got away with destroying us and so many other families always was the major sticking point for Mom.

"When we found out about Victor's affairs, it shattered that for us. I know cheating is a common occurrence, but that in no way negates the fact that it deeply affects the emotional and mental well-being of the people around us. I guess I just expected someone somewhere to come clean about it all." I could see Mom struggle to keep a neutral expression while she relived her pain out loud.

"I can see that there is a lot of hurt there, Maggie. Oftentimes, spouses or children in these situations can have PTSD even. In fact, it's the kids who suffer most sometimes." Amy seemed well versed on the topic. She picked up where Mom left off, sharing her knowledge on the topic. "I know you've had your share of therapy since you found out. I actually work with a lot of people who suffer from emotional flooding. It sounds like maybe that has been you in the past?" Amy gave a half nod for approval at Mom, which Mom validated with one strong nod back.

"I'd just pace and yell at no one, just a downward spiral of cursing and catastrophizing." I could hear the embarrassment in my mom's voice.

"I know Nick has had his share of PTSD, but have his brothers responded the same way?" Amy's inquisition continued to pull the little threads of information out of Mom to piece together our story.

"Nick took it the toughest. Although my middle son is currently working through it in very different ways too."

"I definitely took it the toughest," I said, confirming Mom's statement.

Amy kept her eyes on us and stood up, walking to her bookshelf across her office where a slew of books stood snuggled next to one another. She placed her pointer finger on the spine of one yellow book and drew it toward her, then handed the book to Mom.

"I love this book." Amy's voice was warm and soothing. "It talks all about what you're saying. Infidelity shocks the brain and causes permanent damage to certain areas. In fact, your vigilance center sees these types of traumas as attacks, and the brain sort of goes on high alert in order to protect you from future pain. Maggie, what you and your family have gone through was absolutely traumatic. I just want to validate that for you."

Amy continued, but in another direction this time. Mom had had enough time on the podium talking about her pain. It was my turn.

"Maggie?" Amy grounded mom with a change of tone. "I know you and Nicholas are really close. Nick has been working hard implementing some techniques that we teach here to get his anxiety under control, but we still feel like some of his connection to family is missing at this point. That's why we felt so strongly that you came when you did. He and I have been talking about needing to feel the support of you and his father together."

Amy's gaze stayed on Mom. Mom took a deep inhale as she foresaw a more mature type of confrontation emerge out of me. "Asking for help is a big part of the healing process. Healing happens in connection with others, so I'm going to ask him to exercise this new skill of asking. Nick, what would you like to ask from your mom?"

Suddenly, I felt light-headed. It was just Mom, but now being asked to use my voice in a way that felt like I was taking care of myself solo brought up all of my fear. "Mom, I'm so happy you are here to help support me. I'm scared to go back to the academy. I'm scared I'll mess up again or that I won't be able to beat my anxiety. I'm scared I won't be strong enough in those moments when I feel it coming and I'll be out of control. I can't risk getting kicked out of the academy. This is my dream." My throat tightened into a dried desert as I spoke. It was still tough to ask for what I needed. I tried to swallow but couldn't. I forced myself to concentrate on the words that I needed to come out of my mouth. "Mom, I need you to move forward without Dad always being an issue. It puts too much stress on me. I need you and Dad to find a way to either work together or work completely apart. I'm sick of the toxic in-between."

I'd never delivered such truths in such a calm manner before. I sat in awe of my own growth. Where there was a muffled voice before, now there was a strong, capable one. Where there was a kid who was used to shutting up and baring the discomfort, there now was the ability to clearly ask for what I needed. I found myself sitting up a bit straighter in my chair as feelings of pride and confidence spilled out of me for once.

Amy gave me a quick *attaboy* wink and refocused on Mom with compassionate eyes. I couldn't help but wonder if infidelity had twisted Amy's world like it had ours.

"Mom, it's been a very difficult past couple of years, but it's time that we have one last hoorah and move forward, yeah? So let's have it."

Mom cleared her throat. "The day that I got the call that Nick was in the ER with rhabdo, I had just come back from Mass. A member of our parish had committed suicide because he found out his wife cheated on him, and we were having a vigil for him. His name was Malik. He was from Senegal. He owned this gym and trained all these people in our town. You know, one of those guys who believed in taking massive action, like a Tony Robbins type. He was only thirty-six, and he killed himself. About sixty of us stood outside, each with a white balloon in our hand, as Father Dabney offered a prayer. We all slowly released our balloons to the sky."

It was as if Amy had been holding the heavy emotions of Mom's story in her body. Now her long exhale released them and gave me permission to do the same.

Mom became choked up through choppy sentences as she continued. "I watched the balloons float up and disappear into the sky. I realized that really could have been me, Nick." She faced me with a seriousness I hadn't seen from her in a while. Then she looked back at Amy. "That could have been one of my boys. Malik took his own life because the truth of his wife cheating on him was so painful, he couldn't bear it. Of course I will, Nick. Of course I will. You know I will do anything for you. It's time to move forward."

Amy nodded her head slowly as if to say, "I know." Two words that summed up practically everyone's motto in this room today.

With those two words, Amy had confirmed the indigestible truth: that infidelity affects everyone, that cheating destroys children's lives, that it's something that happens every day but is rarely talked about, and that no one is held accountable with their friends and family. I mean, Dad had made us the laughingstock of our little all-American town. Everyone seemed to know his dirty little secrets, yet he was the one still banging every woman who'd let him. Amy reached out her hand to Mom. Mom draped her fingers inside Amy's palm, where it was held safely. There was so much heartbreak lingering in the air in that room where the three of us sat. I stifled back the natural reflex to release a few tears, while Mom and Amy shared a few cleansing tears together. I let them have their moment.

"This isn't easy." Amy's eyes were full of compassion. "Believe me, I know. Nick has been in good hands and good company here while processing this trauma, if you know what I mean. This is something that affects everyone, not just wives."

Mom wiped her tears away with a wadded tissue that had molded into a ball in her hand.

"Mom," I began, "like, practically everyone in here is affected by it. Manchester cheated on his wife more than a decade ago, and it ruined his life. Chief Drea still won't say much about her experience but said something about an angry husband who came to try to kill her dad for messing around with his wife, and it didn't end well. Phil's wife cheated on him . . ."

I caught the words coming out of my mouth. I couldn't believe there were so many of us, yet it took being in the psych unit for everyone to start talking about it. Suddenly, I noticed how private the topic of infidelity was back home. Everyone walking around with zipped lips about what happens behind closed doors, yet people are literally killing themselves because of it. *Was it more women than men, or more men than women? More whores out there or more douches?* I laughed bitterly to myself.

I imagined what it would be like if all the adulterers were outed in public like in that book I read in eleventh grade, *The Scarlet Letter.* How ironic that while I was reading about adultery through the words of Nathaniel Hawthorne in Mr. Lutz's class, Dad was literally playing out the part in real life . . . many times over. While the movie version showed the unfaithful shamefully wearing the letter A like a badge, those office whores played their parts, wearing their nurse scrubs, carrying their medical files like little props to cover their dirty little secrets: their dumb tales of sleeping with the married doctors, told in their ridiculously annoying mousy voices. Thinking about that sick circle of Dad and the nurses made me want to gag. The phrase "what a jackass" was the only group of words I could conjure up in response to the thought.

Maybe our little middle-American town was reflecting a miniature version of what goes on outside of our bubble. Like hearing about Jeff Bezos being the wealthiest man in the world and then reading articles about his infidelity—with his kids mentioned in the article only as an afterthought. *Yeah, what about those kids? Did they end up in therapy with their mothers or go to psych units for recovery from debilitating anxiety?* Something told me I was one of millions, and I was also ready to move past this now.

Later that day, after a heart-to-heart over the phone, Dad flew in to honor his part in also supporting me. As I made my way down that fluorescent hall for maybe the last time to greet him at the front, I saw him clear on the other end, leaning over the front desk counter chatting up one of the newer nurses. And although I couldn't make out what he was saying, I could see it in his eyes: that sly, half-smile he has when he's flirting, the way his hands gestured dramatically, and the familiar inflections that I'd witnessed him use to get his way so many times over the years. I noticed his hair, usually sloppy, was conveniently styled for the purpose. *What a jackass.*

It was odd seeing him after doing so much investigation into the *hows* and *whys* of his behavior here in the psych ward. Instead of me resenting him, feeling my bottled-up frustration or all of the unanswered questions I'd never had the balls to ask him, surprisingly, I noticed I didn't feel those things at all. I caught myself staring at his outdated jeans, running shoes, and collared knit shirt and him putting on the same old act as before. Maybe it worked when he was younger, but now he was old and creepy. He was an obsolescent compulsive womanizer. Younger and more attractive morons, I'm sure, had already taken his place in our society. Or does it even work that way? Mom and I had done our work to move forward, but for the first time, it became so clear to me . . . Dad never would. He would womanize as long as his bank account had two commas in it.

Mom, Dad, and I said our hellos and headed out for the heart-to-heart over lunch. Amy suggested we have a meeting to discuss how to support me in the next phase of my life. It's funny. Two weeks before, the mere mention of the three of us sitting down to talk face-to-face would have sent me out of or-bit, but this time I felt prepared, excited, and ready to use my voice to ask for what I needed from Dad. Whether or not he could show up for me or could even actually hear what I was saying wasn't the point. I loved him, but Dad was only capable of so much. I knew his limitations, but I wasn't going to let them stop me from claiming my future or asking for his sup-port. Dad was amazing at providing for us. I mean, I had every opportunity in the world. But maybe it was time for me to step up and be a leader in ways that he could not. I was more than ready this time around.

We picked a small, locally famous barbecue joint a couple of miles away from the hospital. It was the kind of place that's a little worn and rough around the edges, and that was part of its charm. Messy food made for the perfect spot in case things got awkward and we needed to stare down at something.

We scooted into a maroon leather booth by the window where the sun faintly shone through. I placed my right hand on the table under the glow of sunshine and felt the warmth radiate up through my palm. There were things I could always trust. Things like where there is sunshine there is also warmth, things like Mom's love, things like my own intuition. I knew I'd be okay. Of course I envied those kids whose parents were still together. I wanted that for us. And of course I wish Dad would have been a stronger man for Mom . . . she deserved it. But I knew I'd be okay, and I knew I was on the right path.

We ordered a ton of food—well, *I* did. Smoked sausage, baby back ribs, marinated pulled pork, three dipping sauces, hush puppies, and cheese grits. I hadn't had this kind of food since I was back home. It was comfort food in the midst of a conver-sation that could easily be highly uncomfortable. I could deal with that. Maybe it was the perfect thing.

"Dad, thanks for coming," I offered gracefully. The words

felt clinical or corporate rolling off my tongue. I felt like I had to say thanks, but I really would have been pleased if Dad were to spontaneously combust. I pushed the thought away, but only because I didn't want my wishes to burn down the restaurant.

"I panicked when I heard you were so sick, bud. I'm happy to see you well. You know you could have called me first, and I would have taken care of it." His words were dry and completely weightless. He was so calm it was eerie, like he had forcibly forgotten everything wrong he had ever done up that point.

"Do you know that you fucked up absolutely everything that you had? You had the perfect family, three superstars, an awesome wife, and you even had shit tons of money. Now you're broke, your kids hate you, and your wife is going to leave you. What's it gonna take for you to pull your head out of your ass?"

"Nicholas, those are *vicious* rumors. Just rumors and gossip." There it was again: his catchphrase to deflect any responsibility. I felt my face get hot as rage built up in me. Part of me was pissed at Mom for staying so silent, but the look on her face was one of total confidence in me. I went on.

"You know what I see, Dad?

"What, Nick?" he said dryly.

"Dad, I see, sitting in front of me, an aged, *pathetic* old man who has lost everything he has, who still won't change. You had everything, then threw it away. You're just a huge con artist. I will never, *never* fall for your crap again and neither will Mom."

He sat there, at least partially stunned, while his narcissism fought to create a shield of hubris and stupidity to protect his sanity. I watched his dry and blank face fake a smile and shake his head, trying to make me look like the villain. It was typical.

I realized I had leaned practically all the way across the table, and the place had gotten quiet while I was putting my dad on blast in front of the entire restaurant. I looked to my sides and saw everyone watching. I glared at them, they turned back around, and the sound came back. I dropped back in my chair and stared back at my Dad.

"You're a failure."

Somehow saying such harsh things aloud sparked the possibility that I might find sadness in Dad's eyes, yet I only saw a bit of disappointment. Nothing else. My mom stared intently at Dad to provide backup.

"I'm going to be a different man than you, Dad. Next year, I'm signing my '2-for-7' commitment at the academy—two more years in school and another five in the fleet. It's not just a job for me or an education or career. It's not about you anymore, and it never should have been."

Out of nowhere, Mom froze and looked at Dad, somewhat extinguishing the inferno that I had started. Time seemed to stop as they locked eyes in some sort of memory. Mom made a slight gasping noise and pointed to the speakers in the ceiling above. "That's right," Mom said in a breath, silently mouthing the words as her shoulders danced to the guitar. "Remember, Victor?" She gave him a nostalgic grin.

And in a moment when I needed it most, Dad looked at Mom for a split second and immediately stared back down at his plate.

"Not really . . ." Dad stated dismissively. (And why would she think that he of all people would make that connection so far in the past?)

"They played this song at our going-away party before we moved. It's Lyle Lovett. We used to play it all the time when the kids were little," Mom explained. "Remember?"

"Mags, you know I don't remember things like that," Dad said and shook his head at her with an awkward smirk to go along with it. My mom just kind of nodded at me as if to say *ouch*.

What a shithead, I thought. I just rolled my eyes. My mom tried to grasp at something human, but I knew it wasn't there. From now on, I would just roll my eyes at his antics and keep calling him out for what he was: a *shithead*. I carefully picked up a rib from my plate. A sweet pink piece of meat hung from the bone . . . for a moment, before I took it between my teeth and devoured it with a smile.

.

11

A LITTLE GRACE

I could almost taste the sweet tang of the pink sherbet sky sprawling out above us in a cool spread as we said goodbye at the front automatic doors of the psych ward. Amy oversaw our obligatory goodbyes in the highest quality representation of the hospital and the academy. While their driver loaded their luggage in the trunk, Mom grabbed her carry-on, monogrammed with her initials, as she and Dad slid into the back of a Lincoln Town Car. I watched the back taillights turn red and bob up and over each speed bump before they made a left turn and disappeared behind the tree-lined street.

It still fascinated me how Mom and Dad had this wild story of betrayal between them, yet Mom could always set aside the issues they had for the sake of us kids. To be honest, they did get along fairly well, if you took the entire marriage out of it, which was even more baffling. After all they've been through, they still hadn't divorced.

It felt like Mom was fighting an internal battle, probably because she was. Mom's heart and brain had some fierce conversations over the years. Never able to finally end this one massive chapter of her life, but knowing she needed to change the game if she was going to survive. Never wanting him close because he disgusted her in his denial, but never wanting him too far because it meant he was out there fucking around. Eventually, Mom joined a recovery group centered around spouses dealing with infidelity, which helped her handle things better and finally do some healing of her own.

After the initial shock of D-Day, when my mom had access to rational thought again, they decided the next best step would be if Dad moved out. Fucking finally. He found a nice apartment behind our gated community. Mom helped him furnish it. A strange thought in me imagined her prepping his apartment for the next woman to come and enjoy. One of those mousy little nurses lounging back in the corner of his L-shaped couch Mom had probably dog-eared in a Pottery Barn catalog, wearing her trendiest leisurewear, reading the trendiest book on the market. The thought always made me want to throw up again. I had to train myself out of thoughts like those that got me all ramped up. Dad had gotten her green light on how he chose to spend his free time. This is where both Mom and I needed to let go of what Dad did and move on with our lives.

I took in the watercolor sky for a moment, grateful for the opportunity to feel more peace for once. Thankful for this psych ward and my time here. Thankful for my lucky childhood and devoted mom, who kept me safe and well-fed. Thankful for Amy and Phil, Manchester, Chief Drea. Thankful that tomorrow morning I was going to be released back into the wild where I'd be asked to be my very best this time around . . . again. This time, I was absolutely confident I could do it. I had the tools this time around. I had the team to help me and now Amy to keep an eye on me. I turned around and headed to my last therapy circle. It was truly bittersweet.

★ ★ ★

As I sat in my last therapy circle, in a chair I'd never picked before, I took a moment to take it all in one last time. One by one, I made eye contact with my friends. Phil, Manchester, Chief Drea, Amy . . . they'd all taught me something valuable in the safe confines of this private room. Drea had inadvertently shown me what true loyalty looks like. Phil managed the lesson of tolerance and surrender . . . even if it was in the most ineloquent form. Manchester helped me see what a real man looks like owning his mistakes and taking responsibility. Amy showed me support and the safety to learn the hard stuff. I loved them all deeply for that.

Walter Reed had been the aircraft carrier that gave me a place to land when I was at thirty thousand feet and running out of fuel with both engines on fire. This hospital had given me a second chance at having the life I dreamed of, but this was my last night in the warm swaddle of support before I entered back into the real world. My belly filled with worry (the low-grade-fever version of anxiety) at the prospect of reentering the academy with grace and confidence after leaving in such a shitshow; after all, that is all I wanted: a little grace.

As I packed the last of my things tightly into my bag and pulled the grommets around each corner to meet in the middle, I closed my eyes for a moment. One of the first skills we learned to reduce anxiety is the "body scan." The idea was to start with the crown of your head, slowly making your way down, just noticing how your body is feeling and different sensations along the way: blood pumping, tightness in your shoulders, tingles in your fingers, etc. I scanned my body. I felt a sense of relief.

Standing here in my familiar uniform felt like I'd circled back to the place I belonged. But I still wondered if I'd be able to able to manage my anxiety better this time around. In fact, the sheer prospect of having another out-of-control episode felt terrifying. If I lost it again, I'd be kicked out for sure. My dreams down the drain. I wondered what my peers thought. I'd only touched base with my roommate twice since entering Walter Reed, but it was still a mystery what the others thought I was doing in here or what was actually going on. I guess I liked it that way.

I hoisted my bag strap over my shoulder with a light groan before opening the door to the hallway where Amy stood to usher me out of Walter Reed and into the van that would take me into the next chapter of my life . . . back to the academy. We reviewed some of my goals as we walked down the corridor and out the double doors. I was finally discharged from Walter Reed.

"Remember, you can do this because you have been doing this." She cheered me on as we strolled at a quick pace.

"I have been doing this. Right," I repeated robotically.

"And you're stronger now. If you feel an attack coming on, you have the skills to handle it this time." She fed me more reassurance, as we approached my van. This was it.

"I wish you the very best, Nick. Will you stay in touch?" she said, pressing her lips together into a tight line just like Mom does. "Stella will drive you. She'll also drop your bags off with your chief at your dorm. That's all been arranged."

"Thank you, Amy. I'll be fine. I'll stay in touch." Against my will, little pinpricks stung behind my eyes, but I shooed them away, gave Amy one last hug, and jumped in the van for the hour-long ride back to the yard. I was ready.

The ride was quick and familiar. We came to an easy stop in a circle drive lined with colorful flowers. The academy was always perfectly landscaped.

Stella just handed me my seabag. Normally, at a college, your stuff would be dropped off with a TA or something, but in the Navy, you're thrown your seabag and figuratively told to go fuck yourself. She wished me well with a Southern drawl.

"Thanks, Stella. Keep my crazy secrets, okay?"

She nodded as I stepped out of the van, showed my ID at Gate 1, the main entrance to the academy, and veered left toward the massive chapel. I've always loved this chapel. It has stood since 1908. Its striking dome (greened over the years) has become one of the trademarks of the Naval Academy. I approached the massive wooden arched doors. Feeling like something else had led me, I wondered, *What am I doing here?* I muscled open one of the doors and tucked myself inside. I allowed myself to be led, knowing something else was in charge in this crazy life.

I tiptoed up the long aisle and to the left as I took in the smells of this hundred-year-old building, until I paused in front of the breathtaking altar to the left of the podium. Around a hundred red votives lined up snug against each other in stadium rows. A few of them burned deep little flames that warmed the air around me.

I reached for a long wooden match. I remembered doing this with Mom at Mass for so many years. I remember her saying something along the lines of "Light it with the other flames. This votive is a symbol of your prayer. When you light your match with the flames of the other prayers, you add to the power of all the prayers. The altar holding our flames becomes one offering to God."

This was the first time I had truly felt the presence of my creator . . . of God in more than a year. I dipped my light wooden match into the flame of the nearest votive and felt the fervor of ignition travel up through my hand. Feeling the confrontation of what to pray for reminded me of birthdays. Memories of Mom cradling Grandma's cake stand with a moist, homemade carrot cake perched on top. Fifteen candles blazing in my face with the command to "make a wish, Nick" echoing through my brothers whose shadows curiously waited for me to close my eyes and blow without a clue what I'd wish for. But this time was different.

This time I was a man, and I knew the prayer in my heart. This one was easy. I let the ping of tears sting the backs of my eyes and spread a warm wave of heat through my cheeks. I held my match humbly upright, then let it bow into one lonely red glass cylinder. I set it aglow. *God give me grace. I need your grace.*

It was my first prayer since I could remember. I surrendered and just let it happen.

I swiftly moved to my first-period class: Leadership and Ethics . . . a class I'd grown quite fond of. I was eager to get back to this particular one, actually. I felt an intuitive draw to the content.

As I approached the regal white brick buildings that crowned the academy, it felt amazing to be back where I belonged, back to the place where I'd build a solid future for myself. I began to climb the stairs to my first period. The first period of this new life: a life I had control over and confidence in.

As I opened the old wooden door, that familiar pungent smell of old books and the warmed plastic blown out by the tiny internal fans from the projector reminded me that I was in the right place. This time my strength wasn't just physical. I was mentally ready for what was next.

12

PURPOSE

Ethics and Leadership . . . I had a new view on the topics of ethics and leadership after a couple weeks in Walter Reed. My internal state had changed, but also my view on the world had changed. I have dreamed of being a surface warfare officer since high school. SWOs are the backbone of fleet leadership, the shot-callers and CEOs of our nation's warships. They loved to say that they were in the business of "putting warheads on foreheads." I wanted that. I wanted to be a SWO fiercely, now that I had emptied my system of everything that stood between the old version of myself and a future that truly made a positive impact. This country needed brave, integral leaders, and I was going to be one of them.

As I made my way to a seat in the far row by the windows, Professor Williams caught my eye. It'd been a couple weeks since I'd been here. It felt right to be back. Professor Williams had that old-fashioned sensibility about him, like Mr. Lutz from high school. The lingering scent of his familiar aftershave hung in the air as I passed by his desk. He gave me a hearty nod with a pleasant smile.

"Welcome back, Newell," he said quietly. He had obviously picked up on my secret desire to be as discreet as possible. "It's great to see you. You look well!"

"It's good to be back, Professor. I feel strong."

Professor Williams allowed for a few more welcome-back greetings from my peers before we officially started class. With only months left of school before plebe year was up, I felt a type of head-down focus settle within me that reminded me that I meant business. I had learned to channel that energy inside of me into meaningful work this time, without it turning into anxiety or breakdowns.

After class, Professor Williams stopped me. "Newell. I wanted to chat with you for a moment, if that's okay."

"Sure. What's going on?" Professor Williams was a serious man and intentional about whom he chatted with after class. This was either really good or really bad.

"I help run a student group once a week in the library. It's centered around mental health." He paused for a moment. "I know you've struggled with anxiety and see that you're really stepping up in this class."

"Both are true, sir." I waited for what came next.

"I'm just throwing this out there, but I wanted to see if you might want to lead a group some time . . ."

"Yes!" I'd answered a little too quickly, but I guess I made it clear that I truly did want it. It was a great way to step up and truly practice my leadership skills. But I was scared. What would people think of me leading a group on something I struggle with on my own? Aren't the experts supposed to be leading these things? Then I remembered what Dr. Ruben said . . . how we should make our struggle our purpose. This would be one hell of a way to do just that.

"Great!" He nodded before I'd fully processed it. "I'll email you some more information. You think you'd be able to lead a group talk next Wednesday?"

"Absolutely," I said with a secret kernel of trepidation. But I had to be honest with myself. I couldn't wait to get back to my room and plan this out.

Walking into my dorm that night felt somehow both invigoratingly new and a little like home. As I opened the door to my room, my roommate Sam and some buddies reared up to greet me.

"Welcome back, fucker!" Sam bellowed . . . a sentiment echoed in chaos around the room.

"Thanks, man." It felt hella good to be welcomed back by my crew.

"You ready for the Herndon Monument climb?" Sam slapped me on the back as he reached for his cell phone.

"Ah, fuck yeah! That's coming up . . ." I'd forgotten in the chaos of returning.

★ ★ ★

That afternoon, as I walked back into my room that still felt new, I closed the door behind me. A small package sat meekly on my desk—a rectangular parcel wrapped in plain brown paper. It was a package from Mom. With curiosity, I tore through to find a box with "Ray-Ban" splayed across the side. Mom always got us boys the good gifts. I slid open the top to find the most beautiful pair of classic aviator glasses. Gold rims, prescription polarized lenses: my eyes widened. Thank God.

Up until now, I'd had to wear what we called "birth control glasses." At least that's what the academy dubbed the government-issued prescription glasses whose style hadn't changed since the mid-1960s. But I had no choice. My eyesight wasn't great, or at least it wasn't perfect. A couple years before, I'd been hit in the left eye with a tennis ball, which caused some damage. Two months later, I'd gotten a disgusting fungal infection after swimming, which further worsened my previously 20/20 sight. Military requirements for eyesight are very strict. Nothing under −6.00 diopters for US Air Force, and nothing under −8.00 diopters for the US Military Academy. I was just a hair under −8.00, so birth control glasses it was . . . until now.

I skimmed off dried shaving cream in the shower as I meditated on the idea of "leading a group." Damn, maybe I wasn't totally ready for it, but I wanted it. It got me thinking . . . maybe no one is ever really fully ready to do new things in their life. How can anyone ever be "fully ready"? Dr. Ruben taught us that if you have a desire, being "ready" is inconsequential. He says, "Forward is forward, whether you're ready or not."

I got dressed, grabbed the books I needed for study group in the library, pulled on my new Ray-Bans, and headed out my dorm doors. The end-of-day sun posed perfectly, greeting me directly in the eye as I hit the bottom stair. Directly behind those deeply penetrating rays stood Walsh. God, I had truly missed her. I pulled down my glasses so I could get a better look at her.

Her name was Hannah Walsh, and I had met her the summer before plebe year at summer seminar—a down-to-earth girl-next-door type I had a hard time calling a "woman," although she was most definitely a woman. Walsh and I just flowed. We had the kind of friendship that I didn't want to mess up by blurring the line that Mom (among many others) often pointed to. And although friendship as the base of any romance was in fact a goal of mine for my next relationship, I wasn't so sure I was ready to mess with my friendship with Walsh. And that's okay. Maybe it was the military uniforms or the male-dominated protocol that stripped women of their feminine beauty, but for whatever reason, the chemistry just wasn't there. Walsh knew I thought she was beautiful and that I loved her in our own buddy kind of way. I never pursued it for more, but I could tell there was a little grain of desire for me inside of her. Maybe there was a part of me that liked that.

"Damn, it's good to see you, Walsh." The words tumbled out of my mouth before I could filter them.

"You look . . . good." She gave me a once-over with her eyes before spinning me around in a little dance. "Dang, Nick! What'd they do to you? You look swole."

Walsh and I had always had a little flirty flare to our relationship. I made her blush. She made me blush. Friends or not, I had forgotten how good it felt to have that attention from her.

★ ★ ★

That Wednesday, as I approached one of the library's second-floor study rooms to lead my first student circle on "Anxiety as a Student," I grinned a little. It was all coming together. To go from struggling with anxiety to leading a student circle about it at the Naval Academy was quite an honor. As I opened the door, more faces greeted me than I had planned on. Peppered in were Walsh, a few familiar peers from class, and . . . Amy. Later she explained that she was working with the Dean in a few meetings that week and felt like dropping in to check on my status. Even though she gave me a kind smile from the back row, it felt as if the wind had been knocked out of me. But I couldn't see her presence as added pressure. I had to focus and lead this like a boss. And that's just what I did.

That first meeting gave me a shot of confidence. I started with telling my story. I'd never told my story before in one concise monologue, but hearing my words spill out into a room of my peers in this vulnerable space felt incredible. As I opened up, they opened up. We connected in our struggles as first-year Naval Academy students in a series of exercises: expressing fears, sharing desires, and practicing mindfulness strategies. Halfway through, I looked around to see six pairs of students partnered up, sharing some of the most difficult things. I couldn't believe I was facilitating this group of people learning to better themselves.

Heading up Wednesday's student circles quickly became a weekly occurrence. First it was a once-a-month thing; then I subbed if Professor Matthews couldn't make the meeting; then

I began cofacilitating or leading them on my own. I felt powerful. I felt like I could help other students who also struggled with anxiety and emotional balance. But that sense of power and service didn't come without its fair share of vulnerability—being blatantly open about my struggles earlier on in the year. I began to feel as if I had found my purpose. Sometimes while I was out on a run, I'd imagine myself backstage, ready to give a TED talk: behind the dark curtain, flipping through my notecards, the edges of the spotlight peeking through under the long velvet drape. On cue, I would step out from behind the curtain, walk right onto that famous red-circle carpet, and begin to speak. Behind me, the words would come up on the screen: "Calm in the Storm: How to Lead Powerfully in the Midst of Chaos."

Then I'd laugh at myself. *You got a ways to go there, buddy.* But somehow, now, it didn't feel impossible.

The rest of plebe year flew by. I settled back in effortlessly. I focused on school like a laser, and even started working in the Naval Academy History Museum. If Luke's thing was baseball, my thing was history. I was a history geek, especially for military history. I couldn't get enough. I found myself quickly immersed in the naval archives down in the library.

Playing around in the pungent odor of antique documents one night after the student rush had died down, I got my hands on some files about Normandy. I'd always been into World War II history. My favorite files were ones on the fact that allied command had known about the mines and the underwater obstacles on the beachhead, and decided on a cost-benefit analysis type of approach. They thought about using RC boats to detonate the mines or divers to try and disarm them, but then they decided that "proceeding forward regardless of the obstacles should not hinder the operation too greatly." They were fine with a couple of the boats getting smacked by the mines, and decided that it would be more economical to allow those men to die than it was to attempt to disarm them. It was chilling, if not spectacularly fascinating. I pretty much declared as a history major on the spot.

* * *

As the end of the school year drew to a close, I realized the Navy Ball was coming up and I still didn't have a date. I knew Walsh secretly wanted me to ask her, and normally I would just to go with someone I knew, but I truly didn't want to give her the wrong impression. Maybe revisiting my dating apps would present some possible options. I was hesitant, though. Mom's friend Anne met a guy on Tinder after her divorce, and for their second date he wanted to have a "pajama party and cuddle," which we all found beyond creepy. Then again, stupid old men usually are creepy if you're finding them on Tinder. I wasn't so sure I wanted to run into the weirdos out there, but I had confidence I could filter them out with more skill than Anne. I grabbed my phone, opened my Tinder app, and started swiping. Let the games begin.

Jen: from San Diego; Boston College, poli-sci major; played soccer; came off a little aggressive in our conversations; not into it. Katie: from Ashburn; University of Maryland, psych major; very cute; right swipe. Heidi: from Germany; Boston College; au pair for family in Boston; tall and just exotic enough to elevate my popularity in an understated way; I'm totally messaging her. Anne Margaret: from Dallas; Yale; ran marathons; she was disciplined; right swipe. They came from all angles, in all shapes, colors, and smarts. Someone for everyone, I guess. In the end, Heidi and I struck up a conversation that I was really into, but I left my proposition up in the air for the time being.

I hadn't seen my sponsor family since before I went to Walter

Reed. One of the things I'd recently learned was the power of connecting to others even when I didn't feel like it. I was even looking forward to a visit. Beth and Bill had called me a couple of times in Walter Reed to check in. They were always so good to me. I figured I'd take a break from the intensity of the academy and make the forty-five-minute drive to visit them for the weekend. It'd feel good to do a little laundry and eat from a real kitchen. I did actually feel comfortable with them.

My sponsor mom, Beth, met me at the end of a flagstone pathway lined with red poppies that led to their giant glass front door. A silver Tesla was parked in the driveway. Beth and Mom had become friends; of course, Mom made friends with everyone. The family was similar to my own. I think the academy matches us up that way. And while I did do my laundry and ate delicious enchiladas with the family, Beth (having heard that I was looking for a date for the dance from Mom) also made arrangements for me to "meet a girl" the next night at a local spot.

As we sat waiting for Caitlyn to meet us for lunch, Beth gave a disclosure that made me wonder why I should be concerned. "She's gorgeous," she said with confidence, then, lowering her voice, continued: "she's . . . curvy . . . but beautiful and smart." Beth handed me her phone with a picture of Caitlyn. She was right. She was curvy and gorgeous. I was never one to equate beauty or attraction with a woman being a size four. I loved a girl who was confident, smart, and that I had an easy rapport with. And while I certainly wanted to pick a date I was attracted to, I cared more about whether we had a connection that could sustain an entire night than if she fit into Gigi Hadid's jeans. But when Caitlyn showed up, I think we were all wondering if we'd been looking at the correct picture of her. Either that picture of Caitlyn on Beth's phone had been photoshopped by a professional modeling agency, or we had the wrong girl. Maybe the pics were just older? The fact that she was much bigger in person than online didn't bother me as much as the misrepresentation and dishonesty. I wanted a woman with integrity, whether she was slender or curvy. Something deep inside felt like this wasn't the right move for now. I got out of there and called Heidi, asking her to the Navy Ball. She said yes, and we had a fantastic time.

Plebe year was coming to a close. With the drama behind me and my confidence building, I was ending the year with flying colors.

Now only one more challenge stood between me and the end of this year: the Herndon climb. For over sixty years—at least, that's when they started timing these events—right before the summer after plebe year, plebes have been gathering around a twenty-one-foot obelisk named for a captain from the 1800s who bravely went down with his ship and his men rather than saving himself.

The tradition goes like this: working together, plebes try to climb this massive marble phallus so that they can replace the plebe cap that upperclassmen have stuck on top with a service cap—the kind we'd all be wearing next year as midshipmen. No wonder this is also called the "plebe-no-more" ceremony.

The catch is that those same upperclassmen have *also* greased the monument with buckets and buckets of lard, making the climb nearly impossible. The plebes have to work together as a team to solve the problem. The best time ever—ungreased— was a minute thirty. When the monument is greased, though, times have gone as long as four hours. I was determined that we'd do better than that.

It was a bright, sunny morning, and the clearing around the monument was surrounded by our classmates, teachers, families, and even townspeople. Most had brought picnics, and all smiled and cheered as we poured in to have our turn at the monster. I was one of the first, and it was crazy to see the plebes behind me just keep coming and coming, a huge mass of us. I started to wonder how we could possibly form a strategy in this chaos. As we ran in, we all ripped off our t-shirts—even the girls, who wore bathing suits underneath—and tossed them at the lard-greased monument, hoping that as they slid down they'd take some grease with them. People started standing on each other's shoulders to try to wipe the monument down with all those white shirts.

In the midst of this chaos, upperclassmen kept spraying us with water, like the rock wasn't already slick enough. Also, a cannon was going off every half hour or so, startling as hell every time.

The lard-wiping efforts went on for a while, with people standing on each other's shoulders, stretching up, sometimes tumbling back into the swarming mass of plebe-flesh below. But you can only get so high standing on people's shoulders. I quickly realized that in order to reach the top of the monument, we'd need a much broader, more solid base.

Some of the other big guys must have had the same realization, because soon a bunch of us were all on our hands and knees at the base of the monument together. Others joined us, more and more, until the base was wide and stable. That's what we needed—I could see it so clearly. If I'd learned nothing else this crazy year, it was that: get a stable base, and you can do anything.

I took a sharp breath: someone's bony knees on sweaty palms were on my back—the second layer was being built. It was okay. I felt good.

Then a third layer—damn, it was getting heavy. I stiffened the muscles in my arms and thighs but tried not to lock my elbows. You don't want to lock up in a situation like this. Stability needs strength and flexibility. Another deep breath. How many layers high were we now? I couldn't guess. How many minutes had passed since I helped form this base—thirty? More?

Now I could feel the bodies above me shifting and moving. A foot on my back as someone climbed. The cannon went off— *BAM*—but I held solid.

Ohhhh! said the crowd. Something was happening—what? Above me, our plebe pyramid rocked, and I heard the thud of a falling body. *Awwww*, moaned the crowd.

I caught a spray of water in my eye. *Thanks, bro.* But I held firm, me and the men around me. We held stable.

For what seemed like an hour, but was probably ten or fifteen minutes, that's all I knew of what was happening above me: the crowd's excited *OHHHHs!!!* and disappointed *Awwwws* as attempt after attempt came close and failed. Once a falling body—must have been coming from ten feet up—hit the guy just above me, and my hand almost slipped from the impact.

But down in the grass and mud, slick with sweat and water and grease, I held stable. We held stable.

Then the cheers and applause started growing. The crowd's energy was getting intense. I figured it out: someone must have gotten high enough to try throwing the hat, because the *Ohhs!* and the *Awwws* were coming every couple of seconds now.

And then without warning, the crowd went wild with cheers. The mass of bodies above me started coming apart, dropping to the ground. When the last sweaty hands and legs came off my back, I leaped to my feet, feeling oddly weightless now, like I was walking on the moon. I looked up, and there it was: the midshipman's cap cocked on the point of the obelisk like it had always been there. My whole class was swirling around me, shouting and cheering, and our friends and families were whooping just as loud for us.

I found out later we'd done it in just over an hour—less than half the time of last year's class. But in that moment, for me, the time didn't matter. We'd worked together. The base had held.

We'd done it. Plebes no more, we'd proved ourselves ready for the next adventure.

Just for a second, I stood still amid the churning crowd. Stable base. My classmates around me. I knew I was ready for anything.

And then, with that knowledge, I gave the loudest, happiest whoop I've ever given and joined the celebration.

ABOUT THE AUTHORS

Alice Rausch is the pen name of a mother of three brilliant boys. As a young woman, her passion for health and justice led her to a career as a health care attorney. As she shifted into the role of a full-time wife and mother, Alice's hands-on approach helped all three children achieve success in sports and academia. Alice currently is seeking a secondary degree in public health and continues to raise her boys with mentorship and love.

Nick Newell is the pen name of the oldest son of Alice Rausch. Nick is a midshipman in the Naval Academy. He plans a career as a naval officer and a life of leadership.